Km

"You're staring at me with bedroom eyes,"

Josh said, frowning

"I am?"

He nodded, looking
I'm little more than a
from job to job shoul

"Why?" She didn't understand his reasoning.

"Because just like that—" he snapped his fingers to emphasize his point "—I'm going to be in and out of your life. I won't see you again after tonight."

"Josh," she whispered, "why do you seem so furious?"

"Because." He stopped and inhaled sharply. "I shouldn't have come to see you tonight, just the way I should never have kissed you."

"I think we should appreciate what we feel for each other and not worry about anything else."

Josh shook his head. "You make it sound so simple."

"And you're complicating everything. If we've only got six and a half hours left together before your plane leaves, then so be it. I can accept that. I don't expect anything more from you, Josh, so quit worrying."

He didn't look any less disturbed, but he did say, "I've been rotten company. I apologize for that."

"Saying goodbye is never easy."

His eyes locking with hers, he murmured, "It has been until now."

Dear Reader,

Welcome to the Silhouette **Special Edition** experience! With your search for consistently satisfying reading in mind, every month the authors and editors of Silhouette **Special Edition** aim to offer you a stimulating blend of deep emotions and high romance.

The name Silhouette **Special Edition** and the distinctive arch on the cover represent a commitment—a commitment to bring you six sensitive, substantial novels each month. In the pages of a Silhouette **Special Edition**, compelling true-to-life characters face riveting emotional issues—and come out winners. Both celebrated authors and newcomers to the series strive for depth and dimension, vividness and warmth, in writing these stories of living and loving in today's world.

The result, we hope, is romance you can believe in. Deeply emotional, richly romantic, infinitely rewarding—that's the Silhouette **Special Edition** experience. Come share it with us—six times a month!

From all the authors and editors of Silhouette **Special Edition**,

Best wishes,

Leslie Kazanjian,
Senior Editor

DEBBIE MACOMBER
Fallen
Angel

Silhouette Special Edition

Published by Silhouette Books New York

America's Publisher of Contemporary Romance

To my aunt, Paula Malafouris,
who taught me that fallen angels
are sometimes the very best kind

SILHOUETTE BOOKS
300 East 42nd St., New York, N.Y. 10017

Copyright © 1990 by Debbie Macomber

All rights reserved. Except for use in any review,
the reproduction or utilization of this work in
whole or in part in any form by any electronic,
mechanical or other means, now known or
hereafter invented, including xerography,
photocopying and recording, or in any information
storage or retrieval system, is forbidden without
the permission of Silhouette Books, 300 E. 42nd St.,
New York, N.Y. 10017

ISBN: 0-373-09577-5

First Silhouette Books printing February 1990

All the characters in this book are fictitious. Any
resemblance to actual persons, living or dead, is
purely coincidental.

®: Trademark used under license and
registered in the United States Patent and
Trademark Office and in other countries.

Printed in the U.S.A.

Books by Debbie Macomber

DEBBIE MACOMBER

hails from the state of Washington. As a busy wife and mother of four, she strives to keep her family healthy and happy. As the prolific author of dozens of bestselling romance novels, she strives to keep her readers happy with each new book she writes.

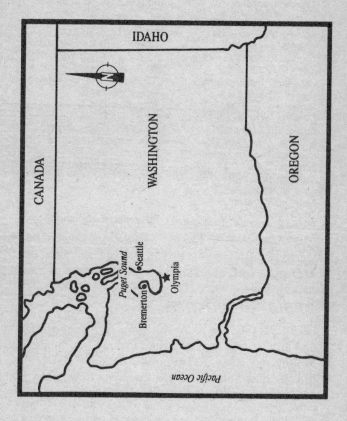

Chapter One

The least it could do was rain! What was the use of living in Seattle if it wasn't going to so much as drizzle? And Amy was in the mood for a cloudburst.

She bought herself an order of crispy fried fish and chips simply because she felt guilty occupying a picnic table in the tourist-crowded pier along the Seattle waterfront. The mild June weather had refused to respond to her mood and the sun was playing peekaboo behind a band of thin clouds. No doubt it would ruin everything and shine full force any minute.

"Excuse me—is this seat taken?"

Amy glanced up to discover a man who looked as though he'd just stepped out of a western novel and was searching for Fort Apache standing opposite her. The impression came from a leather sweatband that was wrapped around his wide forehead and from the cropped-waisted doeskin jacket, complete with a layer of fringe and silver conches.

"Feel free," she said motioning toward the empty space opposite her. "I'll be finished here within a couple of minutes."

"It doesn't look like you've even touched your meal."

"I couldn't possibly eat at a time like this," she said frowning at him.

His thick brows shot upward as he lifted his leg over the wooden table and sat opposite her. "I see."

Amy picked up a fat French fry and poised it in front of her mouth. "I've been home exactly two weeks and it hasn't so much as rained once. This is Seattle, mind you, and there hasn't even been a heavy dew."

"The weather *has* been great."

"I'd feel better if it rained," she returned absently. "It's much too difficult to be depressed when the sun is shining and the birds are chirping and everyone around me is in this jovial, carefree mood."

The stranger took a sip of his coffee, and Amy suspected he did so to cover a smile. It would be just her luck to have a handsome stranger sit down and try to brighten her mood.

He set the cup on the picnic table and leveled his gaze at her. "You look to me like a woman who's been done wrong by her man."

"That's another thing," Amy cried, tossing her hands into the air in abject frustration. "Everything would be so much simpler if I'd been born a male."

Her companion's brown eyes rounded. "Is that a fact?"

"Well, of course, then I wouldn't be in this mess . . . well, I would, but I'd probably be happy about it."

"I see."

Feeling slightly better about the situation, Amy tore off a piece of fish and studied it before popping it into her mouth. It tasted good, much better than she'd anticipated. "It wouldn't be nearly this difficult if I didn't have the most wonderful father in the world."

His dark eyes softened. "Then you shouldn't need to worry."

"But it just kills me to disappoint him." Amy took another bite of the battered fish. "After all, I am twenty-three—it's not as though I don't know what I want."

"And what *do* you want?"

"Hell if I know," she muttered. "No one even asked me before."

Her newfound friend laughed outright at that.

Amy smiled, too, for the first time in what seemed like years. "If I'm going to be spilling my guts to you, I might as well introduce myself. I'm Amy Johnson."

"Josh Powell." He held out his hand and they exchanged quick handshakes.

"Hello, Josh."

"Hello yourself," he returned, grinning broadly. "Are you going to be all right, Amy Johnson?"

She expelled a harsh sigh, then shrugged. "I suppose." Another French fry made its way into her mouth. When she reached for the fish, she noted that Josh had stopped eating and was studying her.

"Is there a reason you're wearing that thick sweater?" he asked.

She nodded. "I was hoping for a downpour—something to coordinate with my mood."

"I thought you might have heard a more recent forecast. An unexpected snowstorm or something."

"No," she admitted wryly.

"Frankly, I'm surprised by the weather myself," Josh stated conversationally. "I've been in Seattle several days now, and the sun has greeted me every morning."

"So you're a tourist?"

"Not exactly. I work for one of the major oil companies, and I'm waiting for government clearance before I head for the Middle East. I should fly out of here within the week."

Her father owned a couple of oil wells, but from what Amy could remember they were in Texas and had been losing money for the past few years. If her father was experiencing minor financial problems with his vast undertakings, then it was nothing compared to what was bound to happen when *she* stepped into the picture. He had such high hopes for her, such lofty expectations. And she was destined to fail. It would be impossible not to. She had about as much business sense as Charlie the Tuna. Her college advisers had repeatedly suggested she change her major. Personally, Amy was all for that. She worked hard and even then she was considered borderline as to whether she would be accepted into the five-year joint BA and MBA program. She'd been number three on a waiting list. Then her father had donated funds toward a new library, and lo and behold, Amy and everyone else on the list had been welcomed into the prestigious school of business with open arms.

"I'm impressed with what I've seen of Seattle," Josh went on.

"It's a nice city, isn't it?" Amy answered with a soft smile. She leaned forward and plopped her elbows on top of the picnic table. "Do you think it would work if I feigned a fatal illness?"

"I beg your pardon?"

"No," she said, answering her own question. "It wouldn't." Knowing her father, he would call in medical experts from around the world, and she'd be forced into making a miraculous recovery.

Josh's amused gaze met hers.

"I'm not making the least bit of sense, am I?"

"No," he admitted dryly. "Do you want to talk about it?"

Supporting her cheek with the palm of one hand, she stared into the distance, wondering if discussing the matter with a stranger would help. At least he would be unbiased.

"My father is probably one of the most dynamic men you'll ever meet. Being around him is like receiving a charge of energy. He's exciting, vibrant, electric."

"I know the type you mean."

"I'm his only child," Amy muttered. "You may have noticed that Dad and I don't share a whole lot of the same characteristics."

Josh hedged. "That's difficult to say—we only met a few minutes ago, but from what I've seen, you don't seem to lack any energy."

"Take my word on this, Dad and I aren't anything alike."

"Okay," he said, then gestured toward her. "Go on."

"I recently acquired my MBA—"

"Congratulations."

"No, please. If it had been up to me I would have hung around the campus for as many more years as I could, applied for a doctorate—anything. But unfortunately that option wasn't left open to me. According to my father, the big moment has finally arrived."

"And?"

"He wants to take me into the family business."

"That isn't what you want?"

"Heavens, no! I know Dad would listen to me if I had some burning desire to be a bricklayer or a dental assistant or anything else. Then I could talk to him and explain everything. But I don't know what I want to do, and even if I did, I'm not so certain it would matter anyway."

"But you just said—"

"I know, but I also know my father, bless his dear heart, would look at me with those big blue eyes of his, and I'd start drowning in this sea of guilt." She paused long enough to draw in a giant breath. "I'm the apple of his eye. According to him, the sun rises and sets on my whims. I can't disappoint him—Dad's got his heart set on me taking over for him."

"You've never told him this isn't what you want?"

She dropped her gaze, ashamed to admit she'd been such a coward. "Not so much as hinted—I just couldn't."

"Perhaps you could talk to your mother, let her prepare the way. Then it won't come as any big shock when you approach your father."

Once more Amy shook her head. "I'm afraid that won't work. My mother died when I was barely ten."

"I see—well, that does complicate matters, doesn't it?"

"I did this to myself," Amy moaned. "I knew the day was coming when I'd be forced to tell him the truth. It wasn't like I didn't figure out what he intended early enough. About the time I entered high school, I got the drift that he had big plans for me. I tried to turn the tide then, but it didn't do any good."

"Turn the tide?" Josh repeated. "I don't understand."

"I tried to marry him off. The way I figured it, he could fall in love again, and his new wife would promptly give birth to three or four male heirs, and then I'd be off the hook. Unfortunately, he was too busy with the business to get involved with a woman."

"What if *you* married?"

"That wouldn't..." Amy paused and straightened as the suggestion ricocheted around the corners of her brain. "Josh...oh, Josh, that's a brilliant idea. Why didn't I think of that?" She nibbled on her lower lip as she considered his scheme, which sounded like exactly the escape clause she'd been wanting. "If my father would be willing to accept any excuse, it'd be something like that. He's a bighearted romantic, and if there's one thing he wants more than to see me in the business—it's grand-children." Her blue eyes flashed with excitement as she smiled at Josh. Then it struck her, and she moaned. "There's one flaw, though." She raised her fingers to her mouth and stroked her lips while she gave the one weakness some thought.

"What do you mean there's a flaw?" Josh repeated, sounding impatient.

"I'm not in love."

"That's not such a difficult hang-up. Think. Surely there's one man you've met in your life that you like well enough to marry?"

"Actually, there isn't," she admitted reluctantly. "I dated in college, but only a little, and there was never anyone I'd seriously consider spending the rest of my life with."

"What about the boys who attended high school with you? Five years have passed, and things have changed— perhaps it's time you renewed those old friendships."

Once more Amy frowned, then regretfully shook her head. "That won't work, either. I attended a Catholic girls' school." She closed her eyes, prepared to mentally scan through a list of potential men she might consider marrying. Unfortunately, she couldn't think of a single one.

"Amy," Josh whispered, "are you all right?"

She nodded. "I'm just thinking. No," she said emphatically, as the defeat settled on her shoulders like a blanket of steel, "there's no one. I'm doomed."

"You could always have a heart-to-heart talk with your father. If he's as wonderful as you claim, then he'll be grateful for the honesty."

"Sure, and what exactly do I say?"

"The truth. You might suggest he train someone else to take his place."

Despite the fact that Josh was serious, Amy laughed a little. "You make it sound so easy... you couldn't possibly realize how difficult telling him is going to be."

"But necessary, Amy."

The second to the last thing Amy needed was the cool voice of reason. The first had been a handsome stranger introducing himself to her. When a person is depressed and miserable, she decided, everything seems to fall apart!

"Talk to him," Josh advised again.

As much as Amy wanted to argue with him, he was right. Her eyes held onto his as if she could soak up his determination.

"The sooner you get it over with the better," he added softly.

"I know you're right," she murmured. "I should do it soon... before I find myself behind a desk, wondering how I ended up there."

"What's wrong with *now*?"

"Now?" Her startled gaze flew to Josh.

"Yes, now."

Her mouth opened to argue with him, but she realized there really wasn't any better a time. The corporate headquarters was well within walking distance, and it would be best to face her father when she was charged with righteous enthusiasm. If she delayed the confrontation until dinnertime, she might chicken out.

"You're absolutely right. If I'm going to talk to my father, I've got to do it immediately." In a burst of zeal, she charged to her feet and offered Josh her hand. "Thank you for your advice."

"You're most welcome." He smiled at her and finished his coffee. "Good luck."

"Thanks, I'm going to need it." Securing the strap of her purse over her shoulder, she deposited what remained of her lunch in the waste basket and marched toward the sidewalk in smooth strides of military precision. When she reached the street, she turned to find Josh watching her. She raised her hand in a gesture of farewell, and he did the same.

An hour later, Amy sat in the back row of the Omnitheater at the Seattle Aquarium, slouched down as far as she could in her seat without slipping all the way out of it and into the aisle. Her hand covered her eyes. A documentary about the Mount St. Helen's disaster was about to start.

Disasters seemed to be the theme of Amy's day. Following her trip to the Rainier Building on Fifth Avenue, she'd walked to the waterfront area where her car was parked. The thought of returning home, however, only added to her misery, so she'd opted for the documentary.

Her fortitude had been strong when she reached the fifty-story structure that housed Johnson Industries. She'd paused on the sidewalk outside and glanced up at the vertical ribs of polished glass and concrete. About half of all the people inside were a part of the conglomerate that made up her father's enterprise.

Her mistake had been when she'd started working with the figures. Calculating two hundred people per floor, that came to twenty thousand workers inside the Rainier Building—when full—of which a possible ten thousand were Johnson employees.

Of all those thousands, only ten or fewer would stand equal to or above Amy in the capacity her father had chosen for her.

She wasn't exactly stepping into an entry-level position. Oh, no, she'd been groomed for a much loftier point on the corporate scale. Her father's idea had been to place her as an assistant, working her way through each of the major sections of the company until the most important aspects of each department had been drilled into her. Naturally, Harold Johnson planned to stay on as president and chief executive officer until Amy had learned the ropes, but "the ropes" felt too much like a hangman's noose to suit her.

The lights lowered in the Omni-theater, and Amy heard someone enter the row and sit next to her.

"I take it the confrontation with your father didn't go well."

Amy's hand flew away from her face. It was Josh. "No," she whispered.

"What happened?"

She flopped her hands over a couple of times, searching for a way to start to explain. "It's a long story."

The man in front of them twisted around and glared, clearly more interested in hearing the details of the natural disaster than Amy's troubles.

"I've already seen the movie once," Josh said. "Do you want to go outside and talk?"

She nodded.

As she suspected, the sun was shining and the sky was an intense shade of blue. Even the sea gulls were in a jovial mood.

"Do you want some ice cream?" Josh asked when they reached the busy sidewalk. He didn't wait for her reply, but bought them each an enormous double-decker cone, then joined her in front of the large, cheerful water fountain.

Amy sat on the edge of the structure, feeling even more pathetic than she had earlier that afternoon.

"I take it you talked to your father?"

"No," she muttered. "I didn't get past Ms. Wetherell, his secretary." She lapped at the side of the cone, despite everything enjoying the rich, smooth taste of the vanilla ice cream. "I don't think I've ever really looked at that woman before. She reminds me of a prune."

"A prune?" Josh repeated.

"She might have been a pleasant plum at one time, but she's been ripened and dried by the years. I think it might be the fluorescent lighting." Amy knew she would look just like Ms. Wetherell within six months. She was going to hate being trapped indoors with no possibility of escape.

"The prune wouldn't allow you to talk to your own father?"

"He was in an important meeting." She turned to Josh and shrugged. "I was slain at the gate."

"Amy..."

"I know exactly what you're going to say, and you're absolutely right. I'll talk to my dad tonight. I promise you I will."

"Good."

He looked proud of her, and that helped. "How'd you happen to be in the Omni-theater?" she asked. It had to be more than coincidence.

"I saw you go inside and was curious to find out what happened."

He'd removed the leather jacket and draped it over his shoulder, securing it with one finger. His eyes were deeply set, his nose prominent without distracting from his strong male features. His ash-blond hair was longer than fashionable, but well kept. It seemed to Amy that calendar and poster manufacturers were constantly searching for men with such blatant male appeal. Men like Josh.

"Is something wrong?" he asked her unexpectedly.

"No," she said, recovering quickly. She hadn't realized she'd been staring quite so conspicuously.

"Your ice cream is melting," he told her.

Hurriedly, she took several bites to correct the problem. The green and white ferry sounded its horn as it approached the pier. It captured Josh's attention.

"Did you know that Washington has the largest ferry system in the world?" Amy asked, in what she hoped was a conversational tone.

"No, I didn't."

"When you consider someplace like the Philippines, that fact is impressive." Amy realized she was jabbering, but she wanted to pull attention away from herself and her problems. "Our aquarium is the only one in the world built on a pier," she said, adding another tour-guide fact. "Have you been up to the Pike Place Market yet?"

"Several times, and I've enjoyed it more each visit."

"It's the largest continuously operated farmers' market in the nation."

"You seem to be full of little tidbits of information."

She smiled and nodded. Then she closed her eyes and expelled her breath in a leisurely exercise. "I really do love this city."

"It's home," Josh said quietly, and Amy sensed such a longing in his voice that she opened her eyes to study him.

"Would you like to walk with me?" he asked her unexpectedly. Standing, he offered her his hand.

"Sure." She linked her fingers with his, enjoying the feeling of being connected with him. Josh had been a friend when she'd needed one. They barely knew each other—they'd exchanged little more than their names—and yet she'd told him more about her problems than she had anyone. Ever. Even her closest college friends didn't know how much she dreaded going to work for her father. But Josh Powell did. A stranger. An unexpected friend.

It took them forty minutes to walk from the waterfront area to the Seattle Center on Queen Ann Hill. They stood at the base of the Space Needle, which had been built for the World's Fair over two decades ago and remained a prominent city landmark. Feeling it was her duty to relay the more important details, Amy told him everything she could remember about the Space Needle, which wasn't much. She finished off by asking, "Where's home?"

"I beg your pardon?"

"Where are you from?"

He paused and looked at her for a tense moment. "What makes you ask that?"

"I . . . I don't know. When I told you how much I love Seattle, you claimed that was because it was home. Now I'm curious where home is for you."

His eyes took on a distant look. "The world—I've taken jobs just about everywhere now. The Middle East, South America, Australia, Europe."

"But where do you kick off your boots and put up your feet?"

"Wherever I happen to be," he returned coolly.

"But—"

"I left what most folks would consider home several years ago. I didn't ever intend to go back."

"Oh, Josh, that's so sad." Her voice sounded as if she'd whispered into a microphone, low and vibrating.

"Amy . . ." He paused, then chuckled softly. "It wasn't any big tragedy." Burying his hands in his pockets, he strolled away, effectively ending the conversation. He paused and waited on the pathway for her to join him.

Glancing at the time, Amy sighed. "I've got to get back to the house," she said with reluctance.

"Tell me what you're going to do tonight."

"Nothing much," she hedged. "Watch a little television probably, read some—"

"I don't mean that, and you know it."

"All right, all right, I'm going to talk to my father."

"And then tomorrow you're going to meet me at noon at the seafood stand and tell me what happened."

"I am?"

"That's exactly what you're going to do."

Her heart started to pound like an overworked piston in her chest, but that could have been because she would soon be confronting her father, and her success rate with making dragons purr was rather low at the moment. But the reaction could well have been to do with the fact that she would be meeting Josh again.

"Any questions?" he asked.

"One." She paused and looked up at him, her eyes wide and appealing. "Will you marry me?"

"No."

"I was afraid of that."

Chapter Two

Manuela had served the last of the evening meal before Amy had the courage to broach the subject with her father. She looked at him, watching him closely, wanting to gauge his mood before she unloaded her mind. His disposition seemed congenial enough, but it was difficult to tell exactly how he would respond to her news.

"Did you have a pleasant afternoon?" Harold asked his daughter, glancing at her.

His unexpected question thumped her out of her musings. "Yes...I took a stroll along the waterfront."

"Good," he said forcefully, and nodded once. Harold Johnson took a bite of his shrimp-stuffed sole and reached for another dinner roll. He was nearly sixty and in his prime. His hair had gone completely white in the past few years, but his features were ageless, as sharp and penetrating as Amy could ever remember. He watched what he ate, was physically and mentally fit and lived life to the fullest. Nothing had ever been done by half measure. Harold Johnson was an all-or-nothing man. There were few compromises in attitude, health or personality.

He was the type of man who, when he saw something he wanted, went after it with everything he had. He would never accept defeat, only setbacks. He claimed his greatest achievements had been the result of patience. If ever he would need to call upon that virtue, it was now, Amy mused. She loved him just the way he was and prayed he could accept her for who she was, as well.

"Ms. Wetherell said you stopped in to see me," he added, when he'd finished buttering his roll.

"You were in a meeting," she answered lamely.

Her father's responding nod was eager. "Damn good one, too. I told a group of executives in five minutes how they can outsell, outmanage and outmotivate the competition."

"You said all that in five minutes?"

"Less," he claimed, warming to his subject. "Mark my words, Amy, because you're going to be needing them soon enough yourself."

"Dad—"

"The first thing you've got to do is set your goals—you won't get any place in this world if you don't know where you're headed. Then visualize yourself in that role."

"Dad—"

He held up his hand to stop her. "And lastly, and this is probably the most important aspect of success, you must learn to deny the power of the adverse. Now you notice, I didn't say you should deny the negative, because there's plenty of that in our world. But we can't allow ourselves the luxury of thinking adversity can get control over us. Because the plain and simple truth is this—misfortune has power only when we allow it to. Do you understand what I'm saying?''

Amy nodded, wondering if she would ever get a word in edgewise and, if she did, how she could possibly say what she must.

''You come to the office tomorrow,'' her father went on to say, smiling smugly. ''I've got something of a surprise for you. I was saving it for later, but I want you to see it now.''

''What's that?''

''Your own office. I've called in one of those fancy interior decorators and I'm having the space revamped. Nothing but the best for my little girl. New carpet, the finest furniture, the whole nine yards. Once that's completed, I want you working with me and the others. Together, you and I are going to make a difference in this country—a big one.'' He paused and set aside his fork. When he looked up, his gaze was warm and proud. ''I've been waiting for this day for nearly twenty years. I don't mind telling you how proud I am of you, Amy Adele. You're as pretty as your mother, and you've got her brains, too. Having you at my side will almost be like having Mary back again.''

''Oh, Dad . . .'' He was making this so much more difficult.

''These years that you've been away at school have been hard ones. You're the sunshine of my life, Amy, just the way your mother always was.''

''I'd like to be more like her,'' she whispered, knowing her father would never understand what she meant. Her mother had always been behind the scenes, acting as a sounding board and offering moral support. That was where Amy longed to be, as well.

Her father reached for his wineglass. "You're more and more like Mary every day."

"Mom didn't work at the office though, did she?"

"No, of course not, but don't you discount her worth to me. It was your mother's support, love and encouragement that gave me the courage to accomplish everything I have done over the years. Never in all that time did Mary and I dream we'd come so far or achieve so much."

"I meant what I said about being more like her," Amy tried once again. "Mom...was more of a background figure in your life and I...think that's the role I should play, too."

"Nonsense! You belong at my side."

"Dad, oh, please..." Her voice trembled like loose change in an oversize pocket. "You just finished telling me how important it was to visualize yourself in a certain role, and I'm sorry, but I can't see myself cooped up in an office day in and day out. It just isn't me. I—"

"You can't what?"

"See myself as an important part of Johnson Industries," she blurted out in one giant breath.

Her announcement was followed by a short silence.

"I can understand that," Harold said.

"You can?"

"Of course. It's little wonder when all you've done, so far is book learning," her father continued confidently. "Business isn't sitting in some stuffy classroom listening to a know-it-all professor spouting off his views. It's digging in with both hands and pulling out something viable and profitable that's going to affect people's lives for the better."

"But I'm not sure that's what I want."

"Of course you do!" he countered sharply. "You wouldn't be a Johnson if you didn't."

"What about Mom, and the support she gave you? Couldn't I start off like that . . . I mean . . . be a sounding board for you and a helpmate in other ways?"

"Years ago that was all you could have done, but times have changed," her father argued. "Women have fought for their rightful place in the corporate world. For the first time in history they're getting the recognition they deserve. You're my daughter, my only child—everything I've managed to accumulate will some day belong to you."

"But—"

"Now, I think I understand what you're saying. I should have thought of this myself. You're tired. Exhausted from your studies. You've worked hard, and you deserve a break. I wasn't thinking when I suggested you start working with me so soon after graduation."

"Dad, I'm not *that* tired."

"Yes, you are, only you don't realize it. Now I want you to take a vacation. Fly on over to Europe and soak up the sun on those fancy beaches. Then in September we'll talk again."

"Vacationing in Europe isn't going to change how I feel," she murmured sadly, her gaze lowered. The lump in her throat felt as large as a grapefruit. She loved her father so much, and it was killing her to disappoint him like this.

"We aren't going to talk about your working until September. I apologize, Amy, I should have realized you needed a holiday. It's just that I'm a bit anxious to have you with me—it's been my dream all these years and I've been selfish not to consider the fact you're in need of a little time to yourself."

"Dad, please listen."

"No need to listen," he said, effectively cutting her off. "I just said we'd talk about it in the fall."

It took everything within Amy just to respond to him with a simple nod.

"You don't understand," Amy said to Josh the following afternoon. "Before I could say a word, Dad started telling me how I was the sunshine of his life and how he'd waited twenty years for this day. What was I supposed to do?"

"I take it you didn't tell him?"

"I did—in a way."

"Only he didn't listen?"

Her nod was slow and reluctant. "It's obvious you've met my father, or at least someone like him. I don't blame Dad—this isn't exactly what he wanted to hear. The best I could do was to admit I couldn't see myself working with him in the office. Naturally, he didn't want to accept that, so he suggested I take the rest of the summer off to unwind after my studies."

"That's not such a bad idea. You probably shouldn't have expected anything more. Frankly, I think you did very well."

"You do?" she asked excitedly, but her mood quickly deflated. "Then why do I feel so rotten?"

"It's not going to get any easier. Last night was difficult, but at least you've gotten yourself a two-month reprieve. Perhaps, in the coming weeks, you'll come up with some way of making him understand."

Amy lowered her gaze and nodded. "Maybe." She raised the cup to her mouth and took a sip of coffee. "What about you, Josh? Did you hear about the government clearance?"

"No—nothing." His voice was filled with resignation.

"I know it's selfish of me," she admitted with a soft smile, "but I'm glad."

"It's easy enough for you to feel that way, you're not the one sitting on your butt waiting."

They shared a soft smile, and Josh brushed a stray strand of hair from her cheek. His fingers lingered as his eyes held hers.

"I'm grateful you came up and asked to share that table with me," Amy admitted. "I was feeling so low and miserable and talking to you has helped."

A short silence followed, before he said, "Actually, I'd been watching you for some time."

"You had?"

Josh nodded. "I waited around for ten minutes to see if someone was going to join you before I approached the table. I was pleased you were alone."

"I wish there was more time for us to get to know each other," she whispered, surprised by how low and sultry her voice sounded.

"No," he countered bluntly, "in some ways it's for the best."

They stood at the end of the pier behind a long row of tourist shops, and Amy walked away, confused and uncertain. She didn't understand Josh. There wasn't anyone else nearby, and when she turned around and looked up, prepared to argue with him, she was surprised by how close they were—only a scant inch or two separated them.

Josh took the coffee from her hand and set it aside. Then he settled his hands on top of her shoulders, and his spellbinding gaze was stronger than the force of her will. His eyes searched hers for a long moment—seeking, probing. She knew then that he intended to kiss her, and her immediate response was pleasure and anticipation. All morning, she'd been thinking about meeting Josh again and her heart had leaped with an eagerness she couldn't fully explain.

With an unhurried ease, he lowered his head to settle his mouth over hers. He was surprisingly gentle. The kiss was slow and thorough, as if rushing something this sweet would spoil it. Amy sighed, and her lips parted softly, inviting him to kiss her again. Josh complied, and when he'd finished, a low moan escaped from deep within his throat.

"I was afraid of that," he said, on the ragged end of a sigh.

"Of what?"

"You taste like cotton candy... much too sweet."

Amy felt a little breathless, a little shaken and a lot confused. In one breath Josh had stated that it was better if they didn't get to know each other any better, and in the next he'd kissed her. Apparently, his mind was just as muddled as hers was.

"Amy, listen—"

"You don't like the taste of cotton candy?" she interrupted, her eyes still closed.

"I like it too damn much."

"Then maybe we should try kissing one more time... you know... as an experiment."

"That might be a bad idea," Josh countered.

"Why?"

"Trust me, it just could."

"Oh," she murmured, disappointed. He placed his fingertips to the vein that pounded in her throat and his thumb stroked it several times as if he couldn't help touching her.

"On second thought," he whispered, a little breathlessly, "maybe that wouldn't be such a mistake." Once more his hungry mouth settled over hers. His kiss was a leisurely exercise as his lips worked from one side of her lips to the other. The heat he generated within her was enough to melt concrete.

He was so tender, so patient, as if he understood and accepted her lack of experience and had made allowances for it. Timidly, Amy slid her hands up his chest and clasped them behind his neck, and when she leaned into him, her breasts brushed against him and her nipples hardened. He must have felt them through her thin shirt because he moaned and reluctantly put some space between them.

Amy struggled to breathe normally as she dropped her flattened hands and braced them against his chest.

"You taste good, too," she admitted. That had to be the understatement of the year. Her knees felt weak, and her heart—well, her heart was another story entirely. It seemed as though it was about to burst out of her chest, it was pounding so hard and fast.

Josh draped his wrists over her shoulders and supported his forehead against hers. For a long time he didn't say a word.

"I've got to get back to the hotel. I have a meeting in half an hour."

Amy nodded; she was disappointed, but she understood.

"Can I see you tomorrow?"

"Yes. What time?" How breathless she sounded. How eager.

"Dinner?"

"Okay."

He suggested a time and place and then left her. Amy stood at the end of the pier, her gaze following Josh for as long as he was within sight, then she turned to face the water, letting the breeze off the churning green waters cool her senses.

With his hands buried deep in his pants pockets, Josh stood at the window of his hotel room and gazed out at the animated city below. His thoughts were heavy, confused.

He didn't know why he was so strongly attracted to Amy Johnson, and then again he did.

All right, he admitted gruffly to himself, she was different. Her openness had caught him off guard. From the first moment he'd seen her, something had stopped him. She had looked so miserable, so troubled. He wasn't in the business of counseling fair maidens, especially blond-haired, blue-eyed ones. Even now he was shocked at the way he'd stood and waited for someone to join her and then did so himself when he was certain she was alone. Somehow, the thought of her being friendless and troubled bothered him more than he could explain, even to himself.

It wasn't his style to play the part of a rescuer. Life was complicated enough without him taking on someone else's problems. He'd convinced himself the best course of action was to turn and walk away.

Then she had looked straight at him, and her slate-blue eyes had been wide with appeal. He had realized almost immediately that although she had been staring in his direction, she wasn't seeing him. Perhaps it was then that he recognized the look she wore. Resignation and defeat flickered from her disturbed gaze. It was like looking in a mirror and viewing his reflection from years past. In

Amy he saw a part of himself that he had struggled to put behind him, to bury forever. And there it was, a look in a lovely woman's eyes, and he couldn't refuse her. He waited for a moment, not knowing what to do, if anything, then he had ordered the fish and chips and approached her table.

Now the travel clearance he had been waiting for had arrived. For the past fourteen days, he had been looking for government approval before he headed for the oil-rich fields of the Middle East. By all rights, he should be taking the first available flight out of Seattle. He should forget he had even met Amy Johnson, with the blue angel eyes and the soft, sweet mouth. She wasn't the first woman to attract him, but she was the first to touch a deep part of himself that he had thought was beyond reach.

In many ways Josh saw Amy as a complete opposite to himself. She was young and vulnerable. The world hadn't hardened her yet, life hadn't knocked her off her feet and walked over her with cleated heels. Her freshness had been retained, and her honesty was evident in every word she spoke.

Yet, in as many ways as they were different there was an equal number that made them similar. Several years back, Josh had faced an almost identical problem to Amy's. He'd loved his father, too, longed to please him, had been willing to do anything to gain Chance Powell's approval.

It was his father's betrayal that had crippled him.

For Amy's sake, Josh prayed matters would resolve themselves differently for her and her father than they had for him and his. He couldn't bear the thought of Amy forced to face the world alone.

Moving away from the view of downtown Seattle, Josh sat at the end of his mattress, where his suitcase rested. The problem was, he didn't want to leave Amy. His mistake had been kissing her. It was one thing to wonder what she would have felt like in his arms, and something else entirely to have actually experienced her softness.

When he had suggested she tell him what had happened once she talked to her father, he had promised himself it would be the last time. Then he had kissed her, and even before he realized what he had been saying, he had suggested dinner. She had smiled at the invitation, and when she spoke, she had sounded so pleased, so eager to see him again.

Only he wouldn't be there. Josh had decided not to show up for their dinner date. It wouldn't take Amy long to figure out that his visa had been approved and he had had to leave. He was being cruel in an effort to be kind. Funny, the thought of disappointing her troubled him more than anything he had done in a good long while.

"Amy," her father called, as she rushed down the curved stairway. "Why are you running like a wild Indian through this house?"

"Sorry, Dad, I'm late," she said with a laugh, because he tended to exaggerate. She hadn't been running, only hurrying. She didn't want to keep Josh waiting.

"Late for what?"

"My date."

"You didn't mention anything about a dinner date earlier."

"I did, at breakfast."

Her father snorted softly. "I don't remember you saying a word. Who is this man you're seeing? Is he anyone I know?"

"No." She quickly surveyed herself in the hall mirror and, pleased with the result, reached for her soft pink jacket, which matched the flowered dress.

"Who is this young man?" her father repeated.

"Josh Powell."

"Powell . . . Powell," Harold echoed. "I can't recall knowing any Powells."

"I met him, Dad, you didn't."

"Tell me about him."

"Dad, I'm already five minutes behind schedule." She grabbed her purse and dutifully kissed him on the cheek.

"You don't want me to know about him? This doesn't sound the least bit like you, Amy. You've dated several young men before, but you've always told me something about them. Now you don't have the time to talk about him to your own father?"

"Dad." She groaned, then realized what he said was partially true. She was afraid he wouldn't approve of her seeing someone like Josh and hoped to avoid the confrontation—a recurring problem with her of late.

Dragging in a deep breath, she turned to face Harold Johnson. "I met Josh on the waterfront the other day. He's visiting Seattle."

"A tourist?"

She nodded, hoping that would satisfy him.

"How long will he be here?"

"I . . . don't know."

Her father reached for a Havana cigar and stared at the end of it as if that would supply the answers for him. "What aren't you telling me?"

It was all she could do not to groan. She was as readable as a first-grade primer when it came to her father in certain areas, while in others he had a blind eye. "Josh works for one of the oil companies—he didn't mention which one so don't think I'm hiding that. He's waiting for his visa to be approved before he leaves."

"And when will that be?"

"Anytime."

Her father nodded, still gazing at his fat cigar.

"Well?" She threw the question at him. "Aren't you going to tell me not to see him, that he's little more than a drifter and that I'm probably making a big mistake? Josh certainly doesn't sound like the kind of man you'd want me to become involved with."

"No. I'm not going to say a word."

Amy paused to study him. "You're not?"

"I raised you right. If you can't judge a man's character by now, you'll never be able to."

Amy was too shocked to say anything.

"So you like this oil worker?"

"Very much," she whispered.

A smile touched the edges of Harold's mouth as he reached for a gold lighter. The flames licked at the end of the cigar and he took two deep puffs before he added, "Frankly, I'm not surprised to discover you met someone. Your eyes are as bright as sparklers on the Fourth of July, and you can't get out of this house fast enough."

"I'd leave now if one cantankerous old man wasn't holding me up by asking me a bunch of silly questions."

"Go on now, and have a good time," he said with a chuckle. "I won't wait up for you."

"Good."

Her father was still chuckling when Amy hurried down the front steps to her car. She felt wonderful. Just when she was convinced her life was at its lowest ebb, she met Josh. He was a cool voice of reason that had guided her through the thick fog of her doubts and worries. She had opened up to him in ways she hadn't with others, and in doing so, she had unexpectedly discovered a rare kind of friend. His kiss had stirred up sensations long dormant, and she held those emotions to her breast, savoring them until she would see him again.

Fifteen minutes after she left home, Amy walked into the French restaurant near the Pike Place Market. A quick survey of the dim interior confirmed that Josh hadn't arrived yet.

Her heart raced with excitement. She longed for him to kiss her once more, just so she'd know the first time had been real and that she hadn't built it up in her mind.

"May I help you?" the maître d' asked when she stepped into the room.

"I'm meeting someone," Amy explained, taking a seat in the tiny foyer. "I'm sure he'll be along any minute."

The man nodded politely and returned to his station. He paused, glanced in her direction and picked up a white sheet of paper. "Would your name happen to be Amy Johnson?"

"Yes," she said and straightened.

"Mr. Powell phoned earlier with his regrets. It seems he's been called out of town."

Chapter Three

Do you mean he's left?" Amy's voice rose half an octave with the question. A numb feeling worked its way from her heart to the ends of her fingertips.

The maître d' casually shrugged his thin shoulders. "All I know is what the message says."

He handed it to her, and Amy gripped the white slip and glared at the few words that seemed so inadequate. "I see," she murmured. Josh might have tried to phone her, but there were a thousand Johnsons in the Seattle telephone directory, and it wouldn't have done him any good, since their number was unlisted. There had been no way for him to contact her one last time and let her know his clearance had arrived.

"Would you like a table for one?" the maître d' pressed.

Amy glanced at the angular man and slowly shook her head. "No. Thanks." Her appetite vanished the moment she realized Josh wouldn't be joining her.

The man offered her a weak smile as she headed for the door. "Better luck next time."

"Thank you." The evening had turned exceptionally dark, and when Amy glanced toward the sky, she noted that thick gray thunderclouds had moved in. "Just in time," she mumbled toward the heavens. "I didn't think it was ever going to rain again, and if I was ever in the mood for it, it's now."

With her hands buried in the pockets of her long pink jacket, she started toward her car, which was parked in the lot across the street.

So Josh was gone. He had zoomed in and out of her life with a speed that had left her spinning in its aftermath, and in the process he had touched her in ways that even now she didn't fully understand.

A smile bounced off her lips as she recalled the first time she had seen him standing above her, holding an order of fish and chips, wanting to know if he could share the picnic table with her. The look in his expressive dark eyes continued to warm her two days later.

She was standing at the curb, waiting for the light to change, when she heard her name carried in the wind. Whirling around, she noticed someone running toward her with his hand raised. Her heart galloped to her throat when she realized it was Josh. Briefly, she closed her eyes and murmured a silent prayer of thanksgiving. Turning abruptly, she started walking toward him, too happy to care that it had started to rain.

Josh was breathless by the time they met. He stopped jogging three steps away from her, and when he reached her, he wrapped his powerful arms all the way around her waist, half-lifting her from the sidewalk.

His hold was so tight that for a second Amy couldn't breathe, but it didn't matter. A consuming happiness erupted from her, and it was all she could do not to cover his face with kisses of pure joy.

"What happened?" she cried when her feet were back on the ground.

The rain was coming down in sheets by this time, and securing his arm around her shoulders, Josh led her into the foyer of the restaurant.

"Ah," the maître d' said, looking pleased. "So your friend managed to meet you after all." He lifted two oblong menus from the holder on the side of the desk and motioned toward the dining room. "This way." His voice took on a formal tone and relayed a heavy French accent that had been noticeably absent earlier.

Once they were seated and presented with the opened menus as if there were insider information from Wall Street to be mindfully studied, Amy looked over to Josh. "What happened?" she asked again. "I thought you'd left town."

His smiling eyes met hers above the menu. "I'm still here."

"Obviously!" She was far more interested in talking to him than scanning the menu. Their waiter arrived and introduced himself as Darrel, as if they should be impressed. Holding his hands prayerfully, he recited the specials of the day, poured their water and generally made a nuisance of himself. By the time he left their table, Amy was growing restless. "Your clearance came through?"

"Yesterday afternoon."

"Then you *are* leaving. When?"

He glanced at his watch as the waiter approached their table once more. "In a few hours."

"Hours," she cried, and was embarrassed when the conversations around them abruptly halted and several heads turned in her direction. Feeling the heat creep into her cheeks, she felt obligated to explain. "I . . . I wasn't talking about our dinner."

A couple of heads nodded and the talk resumed.

"Would you care to place your order?" Darrel inquired, his eyes darting from Amy to Josh and back again.

"No," she said forcefully. "Could you give us ten more minutes?"

"Of course." He dipped his head slightly and excused himself, looking mildly disgruntled.

Amy smoothed the white linen napkin onto her lap as the realization hit her that if Josh was scheduled to depart in several hours, then he must have decided earlier not to meet her. But for some unknown reason, he'd changed his mind. "What made you decide to see me?" she asked starkly.

Josh's eyes clashed with hers, and a breathless moment passed before he answered her. "I couldn't stay away."

His answer was honest enough, but it did little to explain his feelings. "But why? I mean why did you want to leave Seattle without saying goodbye?"

"Oh, Amy." He said her name on the end of a troubled sigh, as if he didn't know the answer to that himself. "It would have been best, I still believe that, but God help us both, here I am."

The look in his eyes caused her to grow hot inside, and she reached for her glass, tasting the cool lemon-flavored water against the tip of her tongue.

"I knew the minute I kissed you it was a mistake." He was frowning as he said it, as though he couldn't help regretting that moment.

"Not a mistake," she said softly, smiling, "fate."

"In any case, I'm flying out of Sea-Tac in a little less than seven hours."

Amy's eyes sparked with eagerness as she leaned toward him. "You mean, we have seven whole hours?"

"Yes." Josh didn't seem to share her excitement.

She set her menu aside. "Are you really hungry?"

Josh's gaze narrowed. "I'm . . . not sure. Why are you looking at me like that?"

"Because if we've got seven hours, I don't think we should waste them sitting in some elegant French restaurant with a waiter named Darrel breathing down our necks."

"What do you suggest?"

"Walking, talking . . . kissing."

Josh's Adam's apple moved up his throat as his eyes bored straight into hers. "None of that. Besides, it's raining." He dismissed her idea with an abrupt look of impatience.

Darrel returned with a linen cloth draped over his forearm, looking more like an English butler than ever.

"I'll have the lamp chops," Josh announced gruffly, handing him the menu. "Rare."

"Escalope de veau florentine," Amy said when their waiter looked expectantly in her direction. She would rather have spent these last remaining hours alone with Josh, but he was apparently going out of his way to avoid that. Twice now, he'd claimed that kissing her had been a mistake, and yet she knew he'd enjoyed the exchange as much as she. In fact he looked downright irritated with himself for having changed his mind about coming this

evening. But he'd professed that he couldn't stay away. He was strongly attracted to her, and he didn't like it one bit.

"Damn it, Amy, would you stop looking at me like that?"

"Like what?" she asked, genuinely confused.

"You're staring at me with bedroom eyes."

He was frowning so hard that she laughed out loud. "I am?"

He nodded, looking serious. "Do you realize I'm little more than a drifter? I could be a mass murderer for all you know."

"But you're not." Their salads arrived and she dipped her fork into the crisp greens.

"The fact that I wander from job to job *should* concern you."

"Why?" She didn't understand his reasoning.

"Because just like that—" he snapped his fingers to emphasize his point "—I'm going to be in and out of your life—I won't see you again after tonight. I don't intend on returning to Seattle. It's a nice place to visit, but I've seen everything I care to, and there isn't any reason for me to stop this way again."

"All right, then let's enjoy the time we have together."

He stabbed his salad with a vengeance. "I don't know about you, but I'm having a fantastic time exactly the way we are."

"Josh," she whispered. "Why are you so furious?"

"Because." He stopped and inhaled sharply. "The problem is, I'm experiencing a lot of emotions for you that I have no right feeling. I should never have come here tonight, just the way I should never have kissed you. You're young and sweet, and most likely a virgin."

Despite herself, Amy blushed.

"Damn," he muttered, setting his salad fork aside and sadly shaking his head. "I knew it."

"That's bad?"

"Yes," he grumbled, looking more put out than ever. "Don't you understand?"

"Apparently not. I think we should appreciate what we feel for each other and not worry about anything else."

"You make it sound so simple."

"And you're complicating everything. You were there for me when I needed a friend. I think you're marvelous, and I'm happy to have met you. If we've only got seven hours—" she paused and, after glancing at her watch, amended the time "—six and a half hours left together, then so be it. I can accept that. When you're gone, I'll think fondly of you and our brief interlude. I don't expect anything more from you, Josh, so quit worrying."

He didn't look any less disturbed, but he returned to his salad, centering his concentration there as if this was his last meal and he damn well meant to enjoy it.

They barely spoke after their entrées arrived. Amy's veal was excellent, and she assumed that Josh's lamb was equally good.

When Darrel carried their plates away, Josh ordered coffee for them both. When the bill arrived, he paid it, but they didn't linger over their coffee.

"The dinner was very good," Amy said, striving to guide them naturally into conversation. "I'm glad you came back, Josh. Thank you."

A smile tempted the edges of his mouth. "I've been rotten company. I apologize for that."

"Saying goodbye is never easy."

"It has been until now," he said, his eyes locking with hers. "You're a special lady, Amy Johnson, don't sell yourself short. Understand?"

Amy wasn't sure that she did. "No," she answered.

"You're far more capable than you give yourself credit for. I don't think your father's as blind as you believe. Once you're in the family business and get your feet wet, you may be surprised by how well you do."

"Et tu, Brute?"

Josh chuckled. "Do you want any more coffee?"

She shook her head.

Josh helped her out of her chair and they left the restaurant.

The rain had stopped for the moment, and a few brave stars poked out from behind a thick cluster of threatening clouds.

With her hands in her pockets, Amy stood in front of the restaurant. "Do you want to say goodbye now?" He didn't answer her right away and, disheartened, Amy read that as answer enough. Slowly, she raised her hand to his face and held it against his clean-shaven cheek. "God speed, Joshua Powell." She was about to turn away when he took hold of her wrist and closed his eyes.

"No," he admitted tightly. "I don't want to say goodbye just yet."

"What would you like to do?"

He chuckled. "The answer would make you blush. Let's walk."

Her nod was eager. He looped her hand in the crook of his elbow and pressed his fingers over her own. Then he led the way down the sidewalk, their destination unknown, at least to her. His natural stride was lengthy, but Amy managed to keep pace with him without difficulty. He didn't seem inclined to talk, which was fine, since there wasn't anything special she wanted to say. It was such a joy just to spend this time with him, to be close to him, knowing that within a matter of hours, he would be gone forever from her life.

After the first couple of blocks, he paused and turned to her. His eyes were wide and restless as they roamed her features, as though setting them to memory.

"Do you want to talk?" she asked, looking around for a place for them to sit down and chat. The area was shadowy, and most of the small businesses had closed for the day. The only illumination available was a dim streetlight situated at the end of the block.

He shook his head. "I don't want to talk," he said evenly, his gaze effectively holding hers. "I want to kiss you."

Amy grinned. "I was hoping you'd say that."

"We shouldn't."

"Oh, I agree one hundred percent. If it was cotton candy the first time, there's no telling what we'll discover the second. Caramel apples? Hot buttered popcorn? Or worst of all—"

He chuckled and silenced her by expertly fitting his mouth over hers. His kiss was so unbelievably tender that it caused her to shiver. His grip tightened, bringing her more fully into the warm circle of his arms. Amy linked her hands to the base of his neck, leaning into him and letting him absorb the bulk of her weight. She strained upward, standing on the tips of her toes, naturally blossoming open to him the way a flower does to the summer sun.

When they broke apart, they were both trembling.

It had started to rain again, but neither of them seemed to notice. Josh threaded his fingers through her hair as he kissed her once more, rocking his lips slowly back and

forth, creating a whole new range of delicious sensations
with each small movement.

He shuddered when he finished. "You're much too
sweet," he whispered, taking a long series of biting
kisses, teasing her with his lips and his tongue.

"So you've said . . . just don't stop."

"I won't," he promised, and proceeded to show her
exactly how much he enjoyed kissing her, expertly using
his tongue, coaxing her to open all the more.

A low moan escaped, and Amy was surprised when she
realized the sound had come from her.

"You shouldn't be so warm and giving," Josh continued, and swept the inside of her mouth with his tongue.
He held her close as if loosening his grip would endan-
ger her life.

Amy felt her knees give. She was a rag doll in his arms.
"Josh," she pleaded, caressing the sides of his face and
the sharp contours of his jawline.

He continued to mold her softness to him and braced
his forehead against hers while he drew in several deep
breaths. Amy couldn't stop touching him; it helped root
her in reality. Her hands cherished his face. She ran her
fingertips up and down his jaw, trying to put the feel of
him into her memory, hoping these few short moments
would last her for all the time that would follow.

"It's raining," Josh told her.

"I know."

"Cats and dogs."

She smiled.

"You're drenched."

"The only thing I feel is your heart." She flattened her
hand over his chest and dropped her lashes at the sturdy
accelerated pulse she felt beneath her fingertips.

"If you don't get dry, you could catch cold," he warned as if he were searching for an excuse to send her away.

"I'll chance it."

"Amy, I can't let you do that." He slipped his arm around her shoulders and guided her east, toward the business-packed section of the downtown area. "I'm taking you to my hotel room. You're going to dry yourself off, and then I'm going to give you a sweater of mine."

"Josh . . ."

"From there, I'll walk you to your car. We'll be in and out of that hotel room in three minutes flat. Understand?"

Her eyes felt huge. He didn't trust himself to be alone with her in his room, and the thought warmed her from the inside out. Amy didn't need his sweater or a towel or anything else, but she wasn't about to tell him that.

By the time they reached the lobby of his hotel, her hair was so wet that it was dripping on the carpet. She was certain she resembled a drowned muskrat.

Josh's room was on the eighteenth floor. He opened the door for her and switched on the light. The suite was furnished with a king-size bed, chair, television and long dresser. His airline ticket rested on the dresser top, and her gaze was automatically drawn to that. The ticket forcefully reminded her that Josh would soon be out of her life. The drapes were open, and the view of the Seattle skyline was sweeping and panoramic.

"This is nice," she said, smiling at him.

"Here." He handed her a thick towel, which she used to wipe the moisture from her face and hair. "What about you?" she asked, when she'd finished.

He stood as far away from her as he possibly could and still remain in the same room. His eyes seemed to be everywhere but on her.

"I'm fine." He scooted past her, keeping well out of her way. His efforts to avoid brushing against her were just short of comical. He seemed to breathe again once he was safely out of harm's way. From the way he was acting, one would suspect she carried bubonic plague. He opened the closet and took out a long-sleeved sweater. "There's a mirror in the bathroom if you need it."

She actually did want to run a comb through her hair and moved into the other room.

"Do you remember the other day when you asked me if I didn't go in to my father's business what I wanted to do instead?"

"I remember." His voice sounded a long way off, as though he was on the other side of the room.

"I've given the question some thought in the last few days."

"What have you come up with?"

She stuck her head around the door. She was right; Josh stood with his back to her in front of the windows, although she doubted that he was appreciating the view. "If I tell you, do you promise not to laugh?"

"I'll try."

She eased his sweater over her head and smoothed it around her hips, then gingerly stepped into the room, hands dangling awkwardly at her sides. "In light of all the advancements in the feminist movement, this is going to sound ridiculous."

"Try me." He folded his arms over his broad chest and waited.

"More than anything, I'd like to be a housewife and a mother." She watched him carefully, half expecting him to find something humorous in her confession. Instead, his gaze gentled and a smile touched the sensuous lines of his mouth.

"I treasure the memories of my mother," she continued. "She was so wonderful to me and Dad, so loving and supportive of everything we did. I've already explained my father's personality, so you know what he's like. Mom was the glue that held our family together. Her love was the foundation that guided him in those early years. I don't know if she ever visited his office, in fact, I rather doubt that she did, and yet he discussed every decision with her. She was his support system, his rock. She was never in the limelight, but she was a vital part of Dad's life, and his business."

"You want to be like her?"

Amy nodded. "Only I'm more greedy. I want a house full of children, too."

Josh's gaze moved deliberately to his watch. "I think we'd better go," he said, sounding oddly breathless.

"Josh?"

He stiffened. "I promised you we'd be in and out of here in a matter of minutes. Remember?"

"I'd like to stay."

"No," he said forcefully, shaking his head. "Amy, please, try to understand. Being alone with you is temptation enough—don't make it any more difficult."

"What about the sweater?" She ran her fingers down the length of the sleeves. "Won't you want it back?"

"Keep it. Where I'm headed it's going to be a hundred degrees in the shade. Trust me, I'm not going to miss it."

"But—"

"Amy!" Her name was a husky rumble low in his chest. "Unless you'd like to start that family you're talking about right now, I suggest we get out of here."

"Soon," she told him firmly, refusing to give in to the shock value of his statement.

Twin brows arched. "Soon?" he repeated incredulously.

"Come here." Her back was pressed against the door, and her heart was pounding so hard that it had long since drowned out what reason remained to her. She had never been so bold with a man in her life, but she knew if she was ever going to act, the time was now. Otherwise, Josh was going to politely walk her to her car, kiss her on the cheek and wish her a good life and then casually stroll away from her and out of her world.

"Amy." His mouth thinned with impatience.

"Say goodbye to me here," she said, smiling, then she motioned with her index finger for him to come to her.

He shoved his hands into his jeans pockets as if he didn't trust them to keep still at his sides. He paused and cleared his throat. "It really is time we left."

"Fine. All I'm asking is for you to say our farewells here. It will be much better than in a parking lot outside the restaurant, don't you think?"

"No." The lone word was harsh and low.

She shrugged and hoped she looked regretful. "All right," she murmured and sighed. "If you won't come to me, then I guess I'll have to go to you."

Josh looked shocked by this and held out his hand as if he were stopping traffic.

The action did more to amuse her than keep her at bay. "I'm going to say goodbye to you, Joshua Powell. And I'm warning you right now, it's going to be a kiss you'll remember for a good long while."

Everything about Josh told her how much he wanted her. From the moment they had stepped into his room the tension between them had been electric. She didn't understand why he was putting up such a fight. For her part, she was astonished by her own actions. Until she had met Josh, she had always been the timid, reserved one in a relationship. Two minutes alone with him and she had turned into a hellcat. She wasn't exactly sure what had caused the transformation.

"Amy, damn it, you aren't making this easy," Josh muttered. "We're playing with a lighted fuse here, don't you understand that? If I kiss you, sweetheart, I promise you it won't stop there. Before either of us will know how it happened, you're going to be out of that dress and my hands are going to be places where no one else has ever touched you. Understand?"

She felt the blood drain out of her face as quickly as if someone had pulled a drain from a sink. Blindly, she nodded. Still it didn't stop her from easing her way toward him.

"By God, I knew it was a mistake to bring you up here." His face was tight, his eyes dark and brilliant. "We're going to end up making love, and you're going to give me something I don't want. Save it for your husband, sweetheart, he'll appreciate it more than I will."

Her heart went crazy. It felt like a herd of charging elephants was stampeding inside her chest. She moistened her lips, and whatever audacity had propelled her into this uncharacteristic role abruptly left her at the threat in his words. Pausing, she drew in a deep, calming breath and forced a smile.

"Goodbye, Josh," she whispered. With that, she turned and bolted for the door before he could see the ready tears that had brimmed in her eyes.

He caught her shoulder and catapulted her around and into the hard cushion of his chest before she made it another step. He cursed under his breath and locked her in

his arms, rubbing his chin back and forth over the crown
of her head in a caressing action, silently apologizing for
shocking her.

"Oh, Amy," he groaned, "perhaps you're right.
Maybe it *is* fate." She felt his warm breath against the
hollow beneath her right ear.

Her head fell back in a silent plea, and he began
spreading warm kisses over the delicate curve of her neck.
With his hands holding each side of her face, he ran his
lips along the line of her jaw, his open mouth moist and
passionate. When she was sure he meant to torment her
for hours before giving her what she craved, he lowered
his mouth to hers, softly, tenderly in a kiss that was as
gentle as the flutter of a hummingbird's wings. A wel-
coming rasping sound tumbled from her lips.

He made a low, protesting noise of his own as his
tongue and lips alternately plundered and caressed hers,
tasting her, savoring her, his mouth so hot and compelling that she felt singed all the way to the soles of her feet.
When they broke apart, they were both breathless.

"Amy... I tried to tell you."

"Shh." She kissed him to silence his objections. She
had no regrets and longed to erase his. "I want you to
touch me... it feels so good when you do."

"Oh, angel, you shouldn't say things like that to a
man."

"Not any man," she whispered, "only you."

Josh inhaled a sharp breath. "That doesn't make it any
better."

"Why don't you just shut up and kiss me again?"

"Because," he growled, "I want so much more." He
ground his mouth over hers as if to punish her for making him desire her so much.

He sought the ripe fullness of her breasts with his fingertips, his touch feather light. Her nipples pearled and throbbed with heat and excitement until she bit into her lower lip at the powerful surge of sensations that assaulted her like a tidal wave. Before she knew what was happening, he had removed the sweater he had given her to wear. His fingers were poised at the zipper at the back of her dress when he paused, his breathing labored. Then, with a supreme effort, he brought his strong loving hands to either side of her face, stroking her satiny cheeks with the pads of his thumbs.

"It's time to stop, Amy. I meant what I said about saving yourself for your husband. I won't be coming back to Seattle."

She dipped her head and nodded, accepting his words. "Yes, I know." Gently she raised her lips to his and kissed him goodbye. But she kept her promise. She made sure it was a kiss Joshua Powell would well remember.

Josh secured the strap of his flight bag to his shoulder and glanced a second time at his watch. He still had thirty minutes before he could board the plane that would carry him to his destination in Kadiri. He had been filled with excitement, eager for the challenge that awaited him in this Middle Eastern country, and now he would have gladly forfeited his life savings for an excuse to remain in Seattle.

His mind was filled with doubts. He had said goodbye to Amy several hours earlier and already he was being eaten alive, caught between the longing to see her again and the equally strong desire to forget they had ever met.

His biggest mistake had been trusting himself alone with her in his hotel room. The temptation had been too much for him, and she certainly hadn't helped matters any. The woman was a natural-born temptress, and she didn't even know it. She couldn't so much as walk across the room without making him want her. All his life, he would remember her leaning against his door and motioning for him to come to her with her index finger. She was so obviously new to the game that her efforts should have been more humorous than exciting. Unfortunately, everything about her excited him.

To complicate matters, she was a virgin. It was just his luck to fall for a virgin. When she started talking about building a secure home life for her husband and wanting children, he knew that she was completely out of his league. They were as different as fresh milk and aged Scotch. She was hot dogs and baseball and freshly diapered babies. And he was rented rooms, a dog-eared passport and axle grease.

He had to bite his tongue to keep from asking her to write him. He didn't often think of himself as noble, but he did now. The sooner he left Amy, the sooner he could return to his disorderly vagabond life-style. However, Josh was confident of one thing—it would be a hell of a long time before he forgot her.

"Flight number 566 will be boarding shortly at gate C-18," the tinny voice of the airline attendant came over the intercom.

Josh checked the flight number on his ticket and stood, collecting his carryon luggage.

"Josh."

He jerked around to discover Amy hurrying down the concourse toward him. For one wild second, Josh didn't know if he should be pleased or not.

It didn't take him long to decide.

Chapter Four

Amy." Josh gripped her shoulders as his hungry gaze scanned hers. "What are you doing here?"

She was still breathless and it took her several moments to speak. "I know I shouldn't...have come, but I couldn't stay home and...and let it all end so abruptly."

"Amy, listen to me—"

"I know." She pressed the tips of her fingers over his lips, not wanting him to speak. He couldn't say anything that she hadn't already told herself a dozen times or more. "I'm doing everything wrong, but I couldn't bear to just let you walk out of my life without—"

"We already said goodbye."

"I know that, too," she protested.

"How'd you know where to find me?"

"I saw your airline ticket on the dresser, and once I knew which airline, it wasn't difficult to figure out which flight you were taking. Oh, Josh, I'm sorry if this embarrasses you.'' She was so confused, hot and cold at the same time. Hot from his kisses and cold with apprehension. She was making a complete idiot of herself, but after weighing her options, she'd done the only thing she could.

"Here," she said, thrusting an envelope toward him.

"What's this?"

"In case you change your mind."

"About what?" His brow condensed with the question.

"About ever wanting to see me again. It's my address and my phone number, and for good measure I threw in a flattering photo of myself, but it was taken several years ago when my hair was shorter and...well, it's not much, but it's the best I have."

He chuckled and hauled her into his arms, squeezing her close.

"You don't have to write," she told him, her voice steady with conviction.

"I probably won't."

"That's fine... well, it isn't, but I can accept that."

"Good."

He didn't seem inclined to release her, but buried his face in her neck and drew in a short breath. "Your scent is going to haunt me," he grumbled. "I'm going halfway around the world and all I'll think about is you."

"Good." Her smile was weak at best. She'd done everything she could by pitching the ball to him. If and when he decided to swing at it, she would be ready.

The voice of the attendant calling out row numbers for boarding purposes was the intrusion that broke them apart. Josh left his arms loosely around her waist. His gaze was as gentle as a caress, and when he brushed his hand across her cheek, his touch was tender, as though he was caressing a newborn baby. "I have to go," he said, his voice low and gravelly.

"Yes, I know." Gently she smoothed his sweater at his shoulders and offered him a feeble smile. "Enjoy the Middle East," she said, "but stay away from those belly dancers."

The next series of rows were announced, followed a minute later by the last boarding call for flight 566.

Glancing over his shoulder at the attendant, Josh edged toward the jetway.

Amy dropped her arms and stuffed her hands inside her pockets for fear she would do something more to embarrass them both. Something silly like reaching out and asking him not to leave, or pleading with him to at least write her.

She did her utmost to beam him a polished smile. If he was going to hold on to the memory of her, she wanted to stand tall and dignified and give him a smile that would make Miss America proud. "Have a safe trip."

"I'm sure I will." He turned and took two steps away from her.

Panic filled Amy—there was one last thing she had to say. "Josh." At the sound of her voice, he abruptly turned back. "Thank you . . . for everything."

"You're welcome."

She nodded, because saying anything more would have been impossible. Ready tears filled her eyes and blurred her vision, ruining the image she was struggling so hard to maintain. Still, she kept her head tilted at a proud angle, determined to send him off with a smile.

"Amy." Her name was a low growl as Josh dropped his flight bag and stepped toward her.

"Go on," she cried, ruining everything by scooting the moisture across her cheeks with the back of her hand. "You'll miss your plane."

He was at her side so fast she didn't have time to think or act. He hauled her into his arms and kissed her with a hunger and need that were enough to convince her she would never find another man who made her feel the things this one did. His wild kiss was ardent, but all too brief to suit either of them.

"Sir," the flight attendant called, standing at the gate. "You'll have to board now—we're ready to depart."

Josh nodded, picked up his bag and started running. No sooner had he entered the belly of the airplane when the door closed and the big-bodied jet rolled away from the gate.

Amy followed its progress, racing along the floor beside the window, hoping to catch one last glimpse of Josh and knowing it was impossible. The plane turned the corner of the building and the taillights faded from sight. For a long moment, Amy did nothing more than stand with her hands pressed against the bright glass, her head demanding that she forget Joshua Powell and her heart claiming the impossibility of such an act.

Harold Johnson was sitting in the library smoking a cigar when Amy quietly let herself into the house. The lights from the crack beneath the door alerted her to the fact her father was up and waiting for her return.

"Hi," she said, letting herself into the room. She sat in the wingback leather chair beside him and peeled off her coat. Slipping off her shoes, she tucked her feet beneath her and rested her eyes.

"You're back."

She nodded. "I saw Josh off at the airport. I gave him my address, phone number and a picture of myself."

"Smart idea."

"According to Josh it was a mistake. I can't understand why he thinks that way, but he does. He made it clear he has no intention of writing me."

"Can you accept that?"

To Amy's way of thinking, she didn't have a choice. "I'll have to."

Her father's low chuckle was something of a surprise. "I don't mind telling you that your interest in this young man is poetic justice."

"Why's that?"

"All these years, there've been boys buzzing around this house like bees in early summer, but you didn't pay a one of them a moment's heed. For all the interest you showed, they could have been made of marble."

"None of them was anything like Josh."

"What makes this one so different?" her father asked, chewing on the end of his cigar.

Amy swore he ate more of it than he smoked. "I don't know what to tell you. Josh is forthright and honest—to a fault sometimes. He's the type of man I'd want by my side if anything was ever to go wrong. He wouldn't back away from a fight, but he'd do everything within his power to see that matters didn't get that far."

"I'd like him, then."

"I know you would, Dad, you wouldn't be able to stop yourself. He's direct and sincere."

"Pleasant to look at, I suspect."

She smiled and nodded. "He wears his hair a little longer than what you'd like, though."

"Hair doesn't make the man." Harold Johnson puffed at the cigar and reached for his glass of milk.

"What are you doing up this late?" she asked after a moment of comfortable silence.

"After we talked when you came home from dinner, I heard you roaming around your bedroom for an hour or two, pacing back and forth loud enough to wake the birds. About the time I decided to find out what was troubling you, I heard you leave. Since I was awake, I decided to read a bit, and by the time I noticed the hour, it wasn't worth going back to bed."

"I'm sorry I kept you awake."

"No problem." He paused and yawned loudly, covering his mouth with the back of his hand. "Maybe I *will* try to get in an hour or two of rest before heading for the office."

"Good idea." Amy hadn't realized how exhausted she was until her father mentioned it.

They walked up the stairs together and she kissed his cheek when she reached her bedroom door. "Sally and I are playing tennis tomorrow morning, and then I'm doing some volunteer work at the center for abused wives later in the afternoon. You didn't need me for anything, did you?"

"No. But I thought you were going to take the summer off?"

"I am," she said, and yawned. "Trust me, Dad, tennis is hard work."

Josh had never been fond of camels. They smelled worse than rotting sewage, were ill-tempered and more stubborn than mules. The beasts were the first thing Josh saw as he stepped off his plane, and he had the distinct impression this country was filled with them. And soldiers. Each and every one of them seemed to be carting a machine gun. So this was the way it was to be. Josh should have suspected as much when he had so much trouble getting his visa.

A cantankerous camel strolled across the runway followed by two shouting men waving sticks and cursing in a language Josh didn't understand.

Joel Perkins, Josh's direct superior and best friend, was supposed to meet him in the crowded Kadiri airport. Kadiri was a tiny country situated between Sudan and Ethiopia, where the company that employed Josh had recently signed a contract for oil exploration and drilling.

The people were poor, undernourished farmers who had yet to receive the benefits from their oil-rich land. Josh wasn't certain how stable the government was, either.

It was like stepping back in time when Josh walked off the plane. The terminal, if the building could be termed that, was filled with animals and produce and so crowded that Josh could barely move.

Ten minutes in this country and already his clothes were plastered to his skin; the temperature must have been over a hundred degrees inside, and no telling what it was in the direct sunlight.

At six foot four, Joel Perkins was head and shoulders above most everyone, so it was easy enough for Josh to spot his friend. Making his way over to him, however, was another matter entirely.

"Excuse me," Josh said twenty times as he scooted around caged chickens, crying children and several robed men who seemed to be praying and repeatedly pressing their foreheads to the ground.

"Good to see you, old buddy," Joel greeted him, and slapped his hand across Josh's back. "How was the flight?"

"From Seattle to Paris was a piece of cake. From Paris to Kadiri . . . you don't want to hear about it, trust me."

Joel laughed. "But you're here now and safe."

"No thanks to that World War Two wreckage that just landed."

"As you can see, the taxis are out of service," Joel explained. "We're going to have to ride into the city on these."

Josh took one look at the ugliest-looking camel he had ever encountered and let out an expletive that would have curled Amy's hair. He stopped abruptly. Every thought that drifted through his mind was in some way connected to her. He hadn't stopped thinking of her for a single minute. Every time he closed his eyes, it was her lips that smiled at him, her blue eyes that flashed with eagerness, her arms that reached toward him.

What he had said to her about her scent haunting him had been prophetic. In fact, he had strolled along the streets of Paris until he had found a small fragrance shop. It took him an hour to discover the perfume that reminded him of her. Feeling like a fool for having wasted the proprietor's time, he ended up buying a bottle. Hell, he didn't know what he was going to do with it. Mail it to his seventy-year-old Aunt Hazel?

"What's the matter, old buddy?" Joel asked. "Has the heat gotten to you already?"

"No," Josh said. "A woman has."

Joel's eyes revealed his surprise. "A woman? Where?"

"Seattle."

"What are you going to do about it?"

Josh didn't need to think before he answered. "Not a damn thing."

Joel expelled his breath in a slow exercise. "Thank God. You had me worried there for a minute."

A week later, Josh changed Joel Perkins's mind.

Exhausted, Amy let herself in the back door of her home. Her face was red, and she wiped it dry with the small white towel draped around her neck. Her tennis racket was in one hand, and after securing it under her arm, she poured herself a tall glass of iced tea.

"Manuela, is the mail here?"

"Nothing for you, Miss Amy," the Spanish-American housekeeper informed her.

Amy tried to swallow the disappointment, but it was growing increasingly difficult. Josh had been gone nearly two weeks, and she'd hoped to hear from him before now.

The phone rang and she left the kitchen. "I'll get it," she called out, stopping in the library to catch the call there. "Johnson residence," she said. Her words were followed by an eerie hum. Amy blinked and was about to hang up the receiver when someone spoke.

"Amy, is that you?"

Her heart raced into her throat. "Josh? Where are you?"

"Kadiri. What time is it there?"

"Three in the afternoon."

"Then I'm lucky to have caught you. I had the times confused. I thought it would be sometime late at night."

He sounded so different. So far away, but that didn't detract from the exhilaration she was experiencing from hearing the sound of his voice.

"I'm so glad you called," she said softly, slumping into her father's desk chair. "I've been miserable, wondering if you ever would. I'd just about given up hope."

"It was Joel's idea."

"Joel?"

"He's a good friend of mine. He claimed that if I didn't call you, he would. Said I had my mind on you when I should be thinking about business. I guess he's right."

"If he were close by, I'd kiss him."

"If you're going to kiss anyone, Amy Johnson, it's me, understand?"

"Yes, sir."

"What's the weather like?"

"Seventy-five and balmy. I just finished playing two sets of tennis. I've been doing a lot of that lately... If I'm exhausted, then I don't think of you so much. What's the weather like in Kadiri?"

"You don't want to know. A hundred and five about ten this morning."

"Oh, Josh. Are you going to be all right?"

"Probably not, but I'll live." There was some commotion and then Josh came back on the line. "Joel's here, and he said I should give you my address so you could write me."

Her heartbeat slowed before she asked, "Is that what you want?"

An eternity passed before he responded. "I don't know what I want anymore. At one time everything was clear to me, but after two weeks, I'm willing to admit I'd be a fool to try to forget you. Yes, Amy, write me. I'll try and get a letter off to you now and again, but I'm not making any promises."

"I understand." She reached for a pen and scribbled down his address, then slowly repeated it to him.

"Listen, I put something in the mail for you the other day, but it'll take a week or more before it arrives—if it ever does. The way everything else goes around here, I doubt that it'll make it through customs intact."

"Something from Kadiri?"

"No, actually, I picked this up in Paris."

"Oh, Josh, you were thinking of me in Paris?"

"That's the problem, I never stopped thinking about you." Once more there was a quick exchange of muffled words before Josh came back on the line. "Joel seemed to think it's important for you to know that I haven't been the best company the last couple of weeks."

Amy closed her eyes, savoring these moments. "Thank Joel for letting me know."

"Be sure and write to tell me if that package arrives. If it does, there's something else I'd like to send you, something from Kadiri." His words were followed by heavy static.

"Josh. Josh," she cried, certain she'd lost him.

"I'm here, but I can't say for how much longer."

"This is probably costing you a fortune."

"Don't worry about it. Joel's springing for the call."

A faint laugh could be heard in the distance, and Amy smiled, knowing already that she was going to like Josh's friend.

"I don't know what the mail will be like coming into the country any more than it is leaving, so if I don't hear from you in a month or so, I'll understand."

"I'll write, Josh, I promise." It was on the tip of her tongue to tell him how much she had thought about him and missed him since he had left. Twice now, she had gone down to the waterfront and stood at the end of the pier where he had first kissed her, hoping to recapture those precious moments.

"I swear living in Kadiri is like stepping into the eighteenth century. This phone is the only one within a hundred miles, so there isn't any way to reach me."

"I understand."

"Amy, listen." Josh's voice was filled with regret. "I've got to go. Joel's apparently bribed a government official to use this phone, and we're about to get kicked out of here."

"Oh, Josh, do be careful."

"Honey," he said, and laughed. "I was born careful."

At that precise moment, the line was severed.

Amy sat down at the dinner table across from her father and smoothed the linen napkin across her lap, feeling warm and happy on the inside.

"So you got another letter from Josh today?"

"Yes," she said, glancing up. "How'd you know?"

"You mean other than that silly grin you've been wearing all afternoon? Besides, you haven't played tennis all week, and before his phone call, you spent more time on the tennis courts than you did at home."

Amy reached for the lean pork roast and speared herself an end cut. "I don't know what tennis has to do with Joshua Powell."

Her father snickered softly. He knew her too well for her to disguise her feelings.

"Little things say a lot, remember that when you start working at the end of the summer. That small piece of advice will serve you well."

"I will," she murmured, handing him the meat platter, avoiding his gaze.

"Now," her father said forcefully, "when am I going to meet this young man of yours?"

"I . . . I don't know, Dad. Josh hasn't written a word about when he's leaving Kadiri. He could be there for several months—perhaps longer. I have no way of knowing."

Her father set the meat platter aside, then paused and rested his elbows on the table, clasping his hands together. "How do you feel about that?"

"I don't understand."

"I notice you're not dating anyone. Fact is, you've been living like a nun. Don't you think it's time to start socializing a little?"

"No." Her mind was too full of Josh to consider going out with another man, although she was routinely asked. Not once in all the weeks since Josh had left Seattle had the thought of dating someone else entered her mind.

Harold Johnson brooded during the remainder of their meal. Amy knew that look well. It preceded a father to daughter chat in which he would tell her something "for her own good." This time she was certain the heart-to-heart talk would have to do with Josh.

Amy didn't have a single argument prepared. Harold was absolutely right, she barely knew Joshua Powell. She'd seen him a grand total of three times—four if she counted the fact they'd met twice that first day and five if she included her harried trip to the airport. It wouldn't have mattered if she'd seen him every day for six months, though. But her father wouldn't understand that. As far as Amy was concerned, she knew everything important that she needed to know about Josh.

When their talk was over, Amy went to her room, took out the letter she'd received and sat on the bed.

Dear Amy,
Your first letter arrived this morning. There are no words to tell you how pleased I was to hear from you. It seems weeks since we talked on the phone, and with Joel standing over me, it was difficult to tell

you the things that have been going through my head. Now, as I sit down to write you, I realize it isn't any easier to put the words to paper. I never was much good with words. I work well with numbers and with my hands, but when it comes to writing letters, I'm at a loss.

I suppose I should admit how glad I was to see you at the airport. The whole time I was waiting for my flight I told myself it was best to make a clean break. Then, all of a sudden, you were there and despite everything, I was so happy you came.

Like I said before, I'm not much good at this letter writing business.

Write again soon.

                                        Love, Josh

Dearest Josh,

The perfume arrived in today's mail. The fragrance is perfect for me. Where did you ever find it? The minute I opened the package, I dabbed some behind my ear and closed my eyes, imagining you were here with me. I know it sounds silly, but I felt so close to you at that moment, as if it was your fingers spreading the fragrance at my pulse points, holding me close. Thank you.

Today was a traumatic one for me. Dad brought me in to work with him to show me how he'd had an office completely remodeled for me. It was so plush, so...I don't know, elaborate. Everything was done in oak. I swear the desk had to be six feet long. I don't suppose this means that much unless you've ever seen my dad's office. He's used the same furniture for twenty years...same secretary, too. At any rate, everything about my dad's office shouts humble beginnings, hard work and frugality. He should be the one with the fancy furniture—not me. I swear the guilt was more than I could bear.

It made me realize that the clock is ticking and I won't be able to delay telling him my feelings much longer. I've got to tell him...only I don't know how. I wish you were here. You made me feel so confident that I'm doing the right thing. I don't feel that anymore. Now all I feel is confused and alone.

Love, Amy

P.S. You haven't been seeing any belly dancers, have you?

Dearest Angel Eyes,

I swear this country is the closest thing to hell on earth. The heat is like nothing I've ever known. Last night, for the first time since I arrived, Joel and I went swimming. We were splashing around like a couple of five-year-olds. The whole time I was wishing it was you with me instead of Joel.

Later I lay on the sand and stared at the sky. The stars were so bright, they seemed to droop right out of the heavens. I had the feeling if I reached up I could snatch one right out of the sky. Gee, I must be getting poetic in my old age. First I'm hanging around looking for the mail every day and happy as a kid in a candy store when a letter arrives from you, and the next thing I know I'm gazing at the stars, wondering if you're staring at them, too. What have you done to me, Amy Johnson?

Joel keeps feeding me warnings. He tells me a woman can be too much of a distraction, and that

I've got to keep my head screwed on straight. He's right. We're not exactly here on a picnic. Don't worry about me, if I'm anything it's cautious.

I put a surprise in the mail for you today. This is straight from the streets of Kadiri. Let me know when it arrives.

Love, Josh

P.S. No, I haven't seen any belly dancers. What about you? Any guys from the country club wanting you for doubles on the tennis courts?

My dearest Josh,
The picture of you and Joel arrived today. You look so tan and so handsome. It made me miss you all the more. I sat down and studied the photo for so long the edges started to curl. I miss you so much, it seems that we barely had a chance to get to know each other and then you were gone. Don't mind me for complaining. I'm in a blue funk today. Dad took me to lunch so I could meet the others from the office and when I arrived home your letter was here.

It made me wish I could sit down and talk to you.

Joel's so tall. I'm pleased he's there with you. Thanks, too, for your vote of confidence in handling this situation with Dad. He seems so oblivious to my feelings. Come September, I probably will move into my fancy new office because I can't honestly see myself confronting him. My fate is sealed.

Your Angel Eyes

It was one of those glorious summer afternoons that blesses the Pacific Northwest every August. Unable to resist the sun, Amy was venting her energy by doing laps in the pool.

"Miss Amy, Miss Amy!"

Manuela came running toward the pool, her hands flying. She stopped, breathless, and a flurry of Spanish erupted from her so fast and furiously that even after two years of studying the language, Amy couldn't make out a single word.

"Manuela," she protested, stepping out of the pool. She reached for her towel. "What are you saying?"

"Telephone . . . long distance . . . man say hurry."

Amy's heart did a tiny flip-flop. "Is it Josh?"

The housekeeper's hands gestured to the sky as she broke into her native tongue again.

"Never mind," Amy cried, running toward the house. By the time she was in the library, she was panting herself.

"Josh . . . Josh, are you still there?"

"God, Amy, who answered the phone? I couldn't understand a word she said."

"That's Manuela. I'm sorry it took me so long. How are you? Oh, Josh, I miss you so much."

"I miss you, too, angel. Your letter arrived yesterday, and I haven't been able to stop thinking about you since."

"I was in such a depressed state when I wrote that . . . I should never have mailed it."

"I'm glad you did. Now, tell me what's happening between you and your father."

"Josh, I can't—not over the phone."

"You're going to work for him?"

"I can't see any way out of it. Are you going to think me a coward?"

"My Angel Eyes? Never."

"I figured the least I could do was give it a try. I don't hold out much hope, but who knows, I might shock everyone and actually be successful."

"You sound in better spirits."

"I am...now. Oh, before I forget, the traditional dress from Kadiri arrived, and I love it. It's so colorful and cool. What did you say the women call it again?"

"Btu-btu."

"I wore it all last night, and the whole time I had this incredible urge to walk around the house pounding drums and singing 'Kumbah Ya.'"

Josh laughed, and the sound did more to elevate Amy's mood than anything in two long months.

"Amy, listen, I've only got a few more minutes. We were able to get use of the phone again, but I don't know how long it's good for so if we're cut off again, don't worry."

She nodded before she realized he couldn't see her gesture of understanding. She closed her eyes to keep the ready emotion cornered. "I can't tell you how good it is to hear your voice."

"Yours, too, Angel Eyes."

She laughed softly to disguise the fact tears were streaming down her face. Hurriedly, she wiped them aside, not wanting him to know. "I loved the picture of you and Joel. Thank you so much for sending it. You look even better than I remember."

"I'm coming back to Seattle."

Amy's head snapped up. "When? Oh, Josh, you don't know how many times I prayed you would."

"Don't get so excited, it won't be until December."

"December," she repeated. "I can wait another five months...easy. How about you?"

"Hell, Amy, I don't know anymore. I've never written a woman before. Half the time I'm so confused by what's happening between us that I can't understand how this company can pay me the money it does. Joel keeps threatening to fire me; he claims he doesn't need anyone as lovesick as me on his crew."

Lovesick. It was the closest Josh had ever come to admitting what he felt for her.

"Hold on a minute," Josh shouted. He came back on the line almost immediately. "Honey, I've got to go. I'm thinking about you, angel—"

"Josh . . . Josh," she cried, "listen to me. I love you."

But the line had already gone dead.

A man could only take so much, Josh reasoned as he walked among the huge drilling structures that had been brought into Kadiri by SunTech Oil. Joel, acting as general foreman, had left his instructions with Josh, but Josh had been running into one confounding problem after another all morning. There wasn't any help for it. Josh was going to have to find Joel and discuss the situation.

It was as he was walking across the compound that he heard the first explosion. The force of it was powerful enough to hurl him helplessly to the ground.

By the time he gathered his wits, men had panicked and were running, knocking each other down, fighting their way toward the gates.

"Joel," Josh cried when he didn't see his friend. Josh searched the frantic, running crowd, but battling through the black workers was as difficult as swimming up a waterfall.

"Joel," Josh shouted a second time, then grabbed a man he recognized by the collar. "Where's Joel Perkins?"

The trembling man pointed toward the building that was belching smoke and spitting out flames from two sides. Something drove Josh forward. Whatever it was had nothing to do with sanity or reason or anything else. The only conscious thought Josh had was the brutal determination to go inside and bring out his best friend.

Two men tried to stop him, screaming a word that Josh found unintelligible. Covering his mouth with a wet cloth, Josh shoved them both aside with a superhuman strength, then, without thought, stormed into the building.

He recognized two things almost immediately. The first was that Joel Perkins was dead. The second was more devastating than the first. The building was going to explode, and there was nothing he could do to get himself out alive.

Chapter Five

Amy."

Her father's gentle voice stirred her from a light sleep. She rolled over onto her back to discover him sitting on the edge of her bed, dressed in his plaid robe, his brow puckered in a dark frown. He'd turned on her bedside lamp to its lowest setting.

"Dad?" she asked, softly. "What is it?"

His eyes pooled with regret, and instantly she knew.

"It's Josh, isn't it?"

Her father nodded. "The call came an hour ago."

Struggling into a sitting position, she brushed the hair from her temples, her hands trembling. She hadn't received a letter in almost two weeks and had already started to worry. Her heart had told her something was very wrong.

"Tell me," she whispered. Her tongue felt thick and uncooperative, but she had to know even if it meant she'd lost him forever. "Is he dead?"

Harold Johnson placed his hands on her shoulders. "No, but he's been seriously injured. There was an accident, an explosion. Five men were killed. Josh wasn't hurt in the initial explosion, but he went back for his friend. Apparently, he was too late."

Amy covered her mouth with her palm and took in deep, even breaths in an effort to curtail the growing alarm that churned in her like the huge blades of a windmill, stirring up dread and fear. "But he's alive."

"Yes, baby, he's alive, but just barely. I can't even tell you the extent of his injuries, only that they're life threatening."

Fear coated her throat. "How did SunTech Oil know to contact me?" Whatever the reason, she thanked God they had. Otherwise, she might never have known.

Her father gently brushed the hair from her brow, his eyes tender and concerned. "Josh listed you as his beneficiary in case of his death. Since he hadn't written down anyone as next of kin, yours was the only name they had. I can't tell you any more than that. The line was terrible, and it was difficult to understand anything of what the official was saying."

Without waiting for anything more, Amy tossed back the covers. "I'm going to him."

Her father shook his head meaningfully. "Somehow I knew you'd say that."

"Then I suppose you also knew I'd want the next flight out of here for Kadiri?" She paused and thought for a moment. "What about a visa?"

"As a matter of fact, I thought of both those things," he admitted, chuckling softly. "There's a connecting plane in Paris, but Kadiri Airlines only flies on Wednesdays."

"But that means I'll have to wait an entire week." She used her thumb and index finger to cup her chin and frowned. "Then I'll get to Paris and hire a private plane to fly me into Sudan. If I have to, I'll walk from there."

"That won't be necessary," Harold told her.

"Why not?" She whirled around, not understanding.

"You can take the company jet. I'm not sending you off to that part of the world without a means of getting you out of there."

Despite the severity of the situation she smiled, tears glistening in her eyes. "Thank you, Dad."

"And while I was at it, I talked to a friend of mine in the State Department. You've been granted a six-week visa, but you won't be able to stay any longer—our relations with Kadiri are strained at best. Get in and out of there as fast as you can. Understand?"

Her mind was buzzing. "Is there anything else I need to know?"

"Yes," Harold said firmly. "When you come home, I want Josh with you."

When Josh awoke, the first thing that met him was pain so ruthless and severe that for a moment he couldn't breathe. He groaned and dragged in a deep breath, trying to come to terms with the fact that he was alive and not knowing how much longer he wanted to live if being so was so damned excruciating. Blissfully, he returned to unconsciousness.

The second time, he was greeted with the same agony, only this time there was a scent of jasmine in the air. Josh struggled to hold onto consciousness. The flower brought Amy to the forefront of his mind. His last thoughts before the building exploded had been of his Angel Eyes, and regret had filled him at the thought of never seeing her again. Perhaps it had been that thought that had persuaded death to give him a second chance. Whatever it was, Josh was grateful. At least, he thought he was, until the pain thrust him into a dark world where he felt nothing.

Time lost meaning. Days, weeks, months could have silently slipped past without him ever realizing it. All he experienced were brief glimpses of consciousness, followed by blackouts for which he was always grateful, because they released him from the pain. The scent of jasmine was in the wind whenever he awoke. He struggled to breathe it into his lungs because it helped him remember Amy. He held onto her image as long as he could, picturing her as she stood at the airport, determined to send him off with a smile. So proud. So lovely—with soulful eyes an angel would envy. It was then that he had started thinking of her as Angel Eyes.

The sound of someone entering his room disturbed his deep sleep. He heard voices—he had several times. They disturbed him when all he wanted to do was sleep. Only this time, one soft, feminine voice sounded so much like Amy. He must have died. But if this was heaven, then why the pain?

"No," he cried, but his shout of protest was little more than a whisper. It wasn't fair that he should fall in love for the first time and then die. Life wasn't fair, he'd known that from the moment he walked out of his father's office, but somehow he'd always thought death would be...

"Josh," Amy whispered, certain she'd heard him speak. It had been little more than a groan, but it had given her hope. "I'm here," she told him, clasping his hand in her own and pressing it to her cheek. "I love you. Do you understand?"

"Miss Johnson," Dr. Kilroy, Josh's English doctor, said with heavy reluctance. "We've only given your friend a fifty percent chance to live."

"Yes, I know."

"He's been unconscious for nearly three weeks."

"I know that, too."

"Please, you aren't helping him by staying at the hospital day and night. Perhaps if you returned to your hotel room and got a decent night's sleep."

"You'll have to get used to my presence, Doctor, because I'm not budging." She turned toward the bed and swallowed back the alarm, as she had every time her gaze rested on Josh. His injuries were multiple, including second-degree burns on his arms, a broken leg, cracked ribs, a bruised kidney and other internal damage, not to mention a severe concussion. Mercifully, he'd been unconscious from the moment she arrived, which had been five days earlier. Not once had she left his side for more than a few minutes. She talked to him, read to him and wiped the perspiration from his brow, touching him often, hoping her presence would relay her love.

The weak sound he'd made just a moment before was the first indication she'd had that he was awake.

"Miss Johnson, please," Dr. Kilroy continued.

"Doctor, I'm not leaving this hospital," she returned sternly.

"Very well," he acquiesced and left the room.

"Josh." She whispered his name and lightly ran her hand across his forehead. "I'm here." His eyes were bandaged, but Dr. Kilroy had assured her Josh hadn't been blinded in the accident.

Another soft cry parted his lips, one so unbelievably weak that she had to strain to hear it. Cautiously, she leaned over the hospital bed and placed her ear as close to his mouth as she could.

"Angel Eyes? Jasmine?"

"At your service," she said, choking back the tears. She didn't know who Jasmine was, but she wasn't going to let a little thing like another woman disturb her now. "You're awake?" It was a stupid question. Of course he was.

"Dead?"

It took her a moment to understand his question. "No, you're very much alive."

"Where?"

"We're here in Kadiri."

Gently, he shook his head and then grimaced. The action must have caused him severe pain. She could tell that talking was an effort for him, but there wasn't anything more she could do to help.

"Where?" he repeated. "Hell? Heaven?"

"Earth," she told him, but if he heard her, he didn't give any indication.

Another twenty-four hours passed before she was able to communicate with him a second time. She had been sitting at his bedside, reading. Since his eyes were wrapped it was impossible to tell if he was asleep or awake, but something alerted her to the fact that he had regained consciousness.

"It's Amy," she said softly, taking his hand and rubbing his knuckles gently. "Here, touch my face."

Very slowly he slid his thumb across the high arch of her cheek. Amy was so excited that it was impossible to sit still. She kissed the inside of his palm. "I love you,

Joshua Powell, and I swear I'll never forgive you if you up and die on me now."

A hint of a smile cracked his dry lips. "Earth," he said and his head rolled to the side as he slipped into unconsciousness.

"Dad," Amy shouted into the heavy black telephone receiver. It made her appreciate the effort Josh had made to contact her by phone, not once but twice.

"Amy, is that you?"

She could almost see her father throwing back his covers and sitting on the edge of his mattress. By now, he would have reached for his glasses and turned on the bedside lamp.

"It's me," she cried. "Can you hear me all right?"

"Just barely. How's Josh doing?"

"Better, I think. The English doctor SunTech Oil flew in says he's showing some signs of improvement. He knows he's alive, at any rate. He's said 'earth' twice now."

"What?"

Amy laughed. "It's too difficult to explain."

"Are you taking care of yourself?"

"Yes . . . don't worry about me."

"Amy." Her father paused and continued in his most parental voice. "What's wrong?"

"Wrong?" she repeated. "What could possibly be wrong? Oh, you mean other than the fact I've flown halfway around the world to be at the deathbed of the man I love?"

"You just told me Josh is improving."

"He is. It's just that . . . oh, nothing, Dad, everything is fine. Just fine."

"Don't try to feed me that. There's something troubling you. Whatever it is—I can hear it in your voice even if you *are* eight thousand miles away. You can't fool me, sweetheart. Tell me what's up."

Amy bit her lower lip and brushed the tears from her eyes. "Josh keeps asking for another woman. Someone named Jasmine. He's said her name three or four times now, and he seems to think I'm her."

"You're jealous?"

"You're damn right I am. I don't even know who she is, but I swear I could rip her eyes out." No doubt she'd shocked her dear father, but she couldn't help it. After spending all this time with Josh, praying he would live, nursing his injuries, loving him, it was a grievous blow to her ego to have him confuse her with another woman.

"Do you want to come home now?"

"Josh can't travel."

"Leave him."

Amy realized the suggestion was given for shock value, but it had the desired effect. "I love him, Dad. I'm here for the long haul. Whoever this Jasmine woman is, she's got one hell of a fight on her hands if she thinks I'm giving Josh up quite so easily."

Her father chuckled, and Amy felt rejuvenated by the sound. It had taken her the better part of three hours to place the call to Seattle, but the time and effort had been well-spent.

"Take care of yourself, Amy Adele."

"Yes, Dad, I will. You, too."

When she returned to Josh's room, she found a nurse and Dr. Kilroy with him. He was apparently in a good deal of pain and was restlessly rolling his head back and forth. Amy walked over to his bedside and clasped his hand between her own.

"Josh," she said. "Can you tell me what's wrong? How can we help you?"

His fingers curled around hers and he heaved a sigh, then apparently drifted into unconsciousness.

"What happened?" Amy asked.

The doctor lifted the patient's chart and made several notations. "I can't be sure. He apparently awoke soon after you left the room and was greatly distressed. He mumbled something, but neither the nurse nor I could understand what he was trying to say. It's apparent, however, that you have a calming effect upon him."

It wasn't until later that night that Josh awoke again. Amy was sitting at his bedside reading. She heard him stir and set her novel aside, standing at his bedside.

"I'm here, Josh."

His hand moved and she laced her fingers with his, raising his hand to touch her face to prove she was there and real and not a disembodied voice in the distance.

"Joel's dead," he said in a husky murmur.

"Yes, I know," she whispered, and her voice caught. Instinctively, she understood that his uneasiness earlier in the afternoon had been the moment he realized his friend had been killed in the explosion.

"I'm so sorry." A tear crept from the corner of her eye and ran down the side of her face. He must have felt the dampness because he lifted his free hand and blindly groped for her nape, forcing her head down to his level. Then he buried his face in the curve of her neck and held her with what she was certain was all the strength he possessed. Soon his shoulders started shaking, and sobs overtook him.

Amy wept, too. For the life that was gone, for the man she never knew, for the dear friend Josh had tried to save and had lost.

She fell asleep that night with her head resting on her arms, which she'd folded over the edge of the mattress. She awoke to feel Josh caressing her hair.

"Good morning," she whispered, straightening.

"Thank you," he returned, his voice still incredibly weak.

No explanation was needed. Josh was telling her how grateful he was that she'd been with him while he worked out his grief for his friend.

She yawned, arching her back and lifting her arms high above her head. "How are you feeling? Are you in a lot of pain?"

"Would you kiss me and make it better if I said I was?"

"Yes," she answered, smiling.

"Amy," he said, his voice growing serious. "You shouldn't be here. God only knows how you got into this country. It took me weeks to get my clearance, remember?"

"I remember." She bent over and kissed his brow.

"Leave while you can."

"Sorry, I can't do that." She pressed a warm kiss along the side of his mouth. "Feel better yet?"

"Amy, please." He gripped her wrist with what little strength he had. "I'm going to be fine . . . you've got to get out of here. Understand?"

"Of course."

"I thought your father had better sense than this. You should never have come."

"Josh, you don't need to worry about me."

"I do . . . Amy, please."

She could tell the argument was draining for him. "All right," she lied. "I'll make arrangements to leave tomorrow."

"Promise me."

"I . . . promise."

Amy could see the tension ease out of him. "Thank you, Angel Eyes."

He seemed to rest after that. Amy felt mildly guilty for the lie, but she couldn't see any way around it.

The following day when Josh awoke, he seemed to know instinctively that she was there. "Amy?"

"I'm here."

"I was afraid of that. What happened? Couldn't you get a flight out?"

"Kadiri Airlines only flies on Wednesday."

"Damn. What day is it?"

"I don't know, I lost track." Another white lie. But the minute he learned it was Tuesday, he would get upset and she didn't want to risk that.

"Find out."

"Dr. Kilroy said he was going to remove the bandages from your eyes today. You don't expect me to leave without giving you at least one opportunity to see me, do you?"

"I'm dying for a glimpse of you," he confessed reluctantly.

"Then I'd better make it worth your while. I have an appointment to get my hair done at eleven." There wasn't a beauty salon within five hundred miles of Kadiri. Josh had to know that.

"Any chance of getting me a toothbrush and cranking up the head of this bed?"

"I'll see what I can do."

It took Amy fifteen minutes to locate a new toothbrush and some toothpaste. Josh was asleep when she returned, but he awoke an hour later. She helped him brush his teeth while he complained about the taste of

Kadiri water. She didn't have the heart to tell him he was brushing with flat soda water.

By the time they'd completed the task, Dr. Kilroy entered the room. The man reminded her of a British Buddy Holly. He turned off the lights and removed the bandages while Amy stood breathlessly waiting.

The minute the white gauze was unraveled from Josh's head, he squinted and rotated his head to where Amy was standing. He held out his hand to her. "I swear, you've never looked more beautiful."

Knowing that after weeks of having his eyes covered, she couldn't be anything more than a wide blur against the wall, she walked to his side and wrapped her arms around his neck. "Joshua Powell, you don't lie worth beans."

He curved his hand around her nape and he directed her mouth down to his. "I've waited three long months to kiss you, don't argue with me."

Amy had no intention of doing anything of the sort.

Josh moved his mouth over hers with a fierce kind of tenderness, a deep, hungering kiss that developed when one had come so terribly close to losing all that was ever important, including life itself. He shaped and fitted her soft lips to his own, drinking in her love and her strength.

Dr. Kilroy nervously cleared his throat, mumbled something about seeing his other patients and quickly vacated the room. Amy was grateful.

"Josh," she whispered while he continued nibbling at her lips, catching her lower lip between his teeth and tugging at it sensuously before he lay back and rested his head on the pillow. Still he didn't fully release her. He closed his eyes and his smile was slanted, full and possessive.

"Angel Eyes," he whispered. "Dear God, it feels good to kiss you again."

"Yes," she agreed, her own voice pathetically weak.

He brought his hand back to her nape, stroking and caressing, directing her mouth back to his own. Amy held back, fearing too much contact would cause him pain.

"I'm afraid I'll hurt you," she whispered.

"I'll let you know if you do."

"But, Josh—"

"Are you going to fight with me?"

Their mouths were so close that their breaths merged. Amy could deny him nothing. "No..."

"Good."

He touched his tongue to her lips, gently coaxing them open, and when she complied to his unspoken request, his tongue slid gently inside, stroking and caressing her own in sleek reunion.

Shudders of excitement braided their way along her backbone, and her heart was hammering like a machine gun inside her chest. When she flattened her palms against Josh's chest, she noted that his heart was beating equally strongly. The movement was reassuring.

Taking in a deep breath, Josh ended the kiss and rested his forehead against hers. Their mouths were moist and ready, their breaths mingling.

"Go back to Seattle, Amy," he pleaded, running his hands through her hair.

"One kiss and you're dismissing me already?"

"I want you home and safe."

"I'm safe with you."

He chuckled lightly. "Honey, you're in more danger than you ever dreamed. Is that door open or closed?"

"Open."

"Damn," he muttered.

She dipped her mouth to his and kissed him long and slow, taking delight in sensuously rubbing her mouth back and forth over his, creating a slick friction that was enough to take the starch from her knees. By the time they broke apart, she was so weak, she'd slumped against the side of the bed.

"Maybe...I should close it," she said, once she'd found her voice.

"No...leave it open," he said with a sigh as he ran his palms in wide circles across her back as though he had to keep touching her to make sure she was real. "Amy, please, you've got to listen to me."

"I can't," she told him, "because all you want to do is send me away." She leaned forward and pressed her open mouth over his, showing him all that he had taught her in the ways of subtle seduction. "Here," she whispered. "Feel my heart." She pulled one of his hands from her back and pressed it to her chest.

"God, Amy." He sucked in a wobbly breath. Fully cupping her breast with his hand, he lifted it and rubbed his thumb across the crest, seeking her nipple, which pebbled at his first touch.

"Josh, I love you," she said, kissing him once more, teasing him with the tip of her tongue.

"No...you shouldn't...you can't."

"But I do."

He closed his eyes to deny her words, but he couldn't keep his body from responding. He moved his hand and lovingly cupped her chin, then brushed the edges of her mouth. "I can't get over how good it feels to hold you again."

She leaned into his embrace, experiencing a grateful surge of thanksgiving that he was alive and on the mend.

"You promised me you were going to leave," he reminded her quietly.

"Yes, I know."

"Are you going back on your word?"

"No." Eventually she would fly out of Kadiri, but when she did, Josh would be with her. Only he didn't know that yet.

"Good. Now kiss me once more for good measure and then get the hell out of here. I don't want to see you again until I'm in Seattle."

"Josh," she argued. "That could be weeks—"

"Honey, will you stop worrying?" He was exhausted. Resting his head against the pillow, he closed his eyes.

It took him all of two seconds to fall asleep. Carefully, Amy lowered the head of his bed, then tenderly kissed his forehead before silently slipping out of the room.

Amy felt better after she'd showered and eaten. From the moment her father had come to her bedside that fateful night all those weeks ago, she hadn't done anything more than nibble at a meal.

She slept better than she had in a month, as well. Waking bright and early the following morning, she dressed in the traditional Kadiri dress Josh had mailed her and walked down to the public market. With her blond hair and blue eyes, she stuck out like a bandaged thumb. Small black children gathered around her, and, laughing, she handed out pieces of candy. The eyes of the soldiers, with rifles looped over their shoulders, anxiously followed her, but she wasn't frightened. There wasn't any reason to be.

Amy bought some fresh fruit and a colorful necklace made from dried and painted seeds and a few other items, then lazily returned to the hospital.

"How's Josh this morning?" she asked Dr. Kilroy when they met in the hallway.

The doctor looked surprised to see her. "He's recovering, but unfortunately his disposition doesn't seem to be making the same improvement."

"Why not?"

The thin British man studied her closely. "I thought you'd left the country."

Amy smiled. "Obviously, I haven't."

"But Mr. Powell seems to be under the impression that you're back in America."

"I let him think that. When I leave Kadiri, he'll be with me."

Dr. Kilroy lifted his thick, black-framed glasses and pinched the bridge of his nose. "Personally, I don't want to be the one who tells him."

"You won't have to be."

"Oh." He paused.

"I'm going that way myself. Is there anything else you'd like me to tell him?"

Dr. Kilroy chuckled, and Amy had the impression that he was a man who rarely laughed.

"No, but I wish you the best of luck with your friend, Miss Johnson. I fear you're going to need it."

With a smile on her lips, Amy marched down the hall and tapped lightly against Josh's door. She didn't wait for a response, but pushed it open and let herself inside.

"I told you, I don't want any breakfast," Josh grumbled, his face turned toward the wall. The drapes were drawn and the room was dark.

"That's unfortunate, since I personally went out and bought you some fresh fruit."

"Amy." He jerked his head around. "What the hell are you still doing here?"

Chapter Six

What does it look like I'm doing here?'' Amy answered, gingerly stepping all the way into the room. ''I brought you some fresh fruit.''

''Dear God.'' Josh closed his eyes against what appeared to be mounting frustration. ''Please, don't tell me you bought that in the public market.''

''All right,'' she answered matter of factly. She brought out a small plastic knife and scored the large orange-shaped fruit. It looked like a cross between an orange and a grapefruit, but when she'd asked about it, the native woman she'd bought it from apparently hadn't understood the question.

''You *did* go the market, didn't you?'' Josh pressed.

''You claimed I wasn't supposed to tell you.'' She peeled away the thick, grainy skin from the succulent fruit then licked the juice from the tips of her fingers.

''You actually did.''

"Honestly, Josh, I was perfectly safe. There were people all around me. Nothing happened, so kindly quit harping about it. Here." She handed him a slice, hoping that would buy peace. "I don't know what it's called. I asked several people, but no one seemed to understand what I was trying so hard to find out about." She smiled at the memory of her antics, her attempts to communicate with her hands, which were no doubt humorous to anyone watching.

Josh accepted the slice. "It's an orange."

"An *orange*? You mean I flew halfway around the world and thought I was buying some exotic fruit only to discover it's an orange? But it's so big."

"They grow that way here."

She found that amusing even if Josh didn't. She continued to peel away the skin and divided the sections between them. After savoring three or four of the sweet-tasting slices, she noted that Josh hadn't sampled a single one of his.

"You promised me you were leaving Kadiri," he said, his words sharp with impatience. His eyes were dark and filled with frustrated concern.

"I am."

"When?"

She sighed and crossed her long legs. "When you're ready to travel, which according to Dr. Kilroy won't be for another two weeks, perhaps longer. Josh, please try to understand, you've received several serious injuries. It's going to take time, so you might as well be tolerant."

"Amy—"

"Nothing you can say or do is going to change my mind, Joshua Powell. Nothing. So you might as well be gracious enough to accept that I'm not leaving Kadiri unless you're with me."

Joshua shut his eyes so tightly that barbed crow's feet marked the edges of his eyes. "How in God's name did you ever get to be so stubborn?"

"I don't know." She wiped the juice from her chin with the back of her hand. "I'm usually not, at least I don't think I am, it's just that this is something I feel strongly about."

"So do I," he returned vehemently.

"Yes, I know. I guess there's only one solution."

"You're leaving!"

"Right," she agreed amicably enough. "But you're coming with me."

Amy could see that she was trying his patience to the limit. His tan jaw was pale with barely suppressed agitation and exasperation. If there had been anything she could do to comply with his demands, she would have done it, but Josh was as obstinate as she, only this time she was fortunate enough to have the upper hand. He couldn't very well force her out of the country.

In a burst of annoyance, Josh threw aside the sheet.

"Josh," she cried in alarm, leaping to her feet, "what are you doing?"

"Getting out of bed."

"But you can't...your leg's broken and you're hooked up to all these bottles. Josh, please, you're going to hurt yourself."

"You're not giving me any choice." The abrupt movements were obviously causing him a good deal of pain. His face went gray with it.

"Josh, please," she cried, his agony causing her own. Gently she pressed her hands against his shoulders, forcing him down. Tears welled in her eyes, and she bit into her lower lip with such force that she drew blood.

Josh's breathing was labored, and certain that he'd done something to harm himself, she hurried down the hall to find Dr. Kilroy.

The doctor returned with her to Josh's room. Almost immediately he gave Josh a shot to ease the pain and warned them both against such foolishness. Within minutes, Josh was asleep and resting relatively comfortably.

Amy felt terrible. When Dr. Kilroy invited her to have tea with him, she accepted, wiping the tearstains from her face.

"Josh seems to think my life is in imminent danger," she confessed. "He wants me out of the country." She stared into the steaming cup of tea, her gaze avoiding his. Even if the doctor agreed with Josh, she was bound and determined not to leave Kadiri unless Josh was at her side.

The good doctor, fortyish and graying, pushed his glasses up the bridge of his nose as if the action would guide his words. "Personally, I understand his concern. This is no place for an American woman on her own."

"But I just can't leave Josh here," she protested. "Are you sure it's going to be two more weeks before he can travel comfortably?"

"Three." He added a small amount of milk to his tea and stirred it in as if he were dissolving concrete. "It'll be at least that long, perhaps longer before he can sit for any length of time."

"What about laying down?"

"Oh, there wouldn't be any problem with that, but there aren't any airlines that provide hospital beds as a part of their flying options," he said dryly.

"But we could put a bed in my father's jet. I flew into Kadiri in a private plane," she rushed to explain. "It's at my disposal for the return trip as well."

Propping his elbows against the tabletop, Dr. Kilroy nodded slowly, thoughtfully. "That changes matters considerably. I think you might have stumbled upon a solution."

"But what about when we land in Seattle? Will Josh require further hospital care?"

"Oh, yes. Your friend has been severely injured. Although the immediate danger has passed, it'll be several weeks—possibly months—before he'll be fully recovered. For the next two or three weeks it would be far better if he remained hospitalized."

Amy knew the minute Josh was released from the Kadiri Hospital he wouldn't allow anyone to admit him to another one stateside.

"Josh isn't one to rest complacently in a hospital," she explained.

"I understand your concern. I fear Mr. Powell may try to rush his recovery, pushing himself. I only hope he realizes that he could do himself a good deal of harm that way."

"I could make arrangements for him to stay at my family home," she offered hopefully. "Would a full-time nurse be adequate to see to his needs? Naturally he'd be under a physician's care."

It didn't take the doctor long to decide. "Why, yes, I believe that would work quite well."

"Then consider it done. The plane's on standby and can be ready within twenty-four hours. Once we're airborne and we can contact Seattle, I'll have my father make all the necessary arrangements. A qualified nurse can meet us at the airport when we arrive."

"I can sedate Mr. Powell so the journey won't be too much of a strain on him . . . or anyone else," Dr. Kilroy added. It was agreed that a nurse would travel with them, although Amy would have preferred it had Dr. Kilroy been able to make the trip with them himself.

"I believe this will all work quite well." The British man looked pleased. "Now, both you and Mr. Powell can have what you want."

"Yes," Amy said, pleased by the unexpected turn of events.

When Josh awoke early in the afternoon, Amy was at his bedside. He opened his eyes, but when he saw her sitting next to him, he lowered his lids once more.

"Amy, please . . ."

"I'm flying out this evening, Josh, so don't be angry again."

His dark eyes shot open. "I thought you said Kadiri Airlines only flew on Wednesdays."

"They do. I'm going by private jet."

His lashes flew up to his hairline. "Private jet?"

"Before you find something else to complain about, I think you should know you're coming with me."

If he was shocked before it was nothing compared with the look of astonishment on his face now. "God, Amy . . . how . . . when . . . why?"

"One question at a time," she said, smiling softly and leaning over him to press her lips to his. "The how part is easy. Dr. Kilroy and I had a long talk. We're flying you to Seattle, hospital bed and all."

"Whose plane is this?"

"Dad's. Well, actually," she went on to explain, "it technically belongs to the company. He's just letting us use it because—"

"Hold on a minute," Josh said, raising his hand. "This jet belongs to your father's company?"

"Right."

His eyes slammed shut, and for one breathless moment he didn't say a word. When he opened them once more, his gaze held hers while several emotions flickered in and out of his eyes. Amy recognized shock, disbelief and a few other ones she wasn't sure she could identify.

"Josh, what is it?"

"Your father's name wouldn't happen to be Harold, would it?"

"Why, yes. How'd you know?" To the best of her knowledge she'd never mentioned her father's first name. But she hadn't been hiding it, either.

The harsh sound that followed could only be described as something between a laugh and a snicker. Slowly, Josh shook his head from side to side. "I don't believe it. And here I thought your father was just some poor devil who wanted to make you a part of a wholesale plumbing business."

Josh wasn't making the least bit of sense. Perhaps it was the medication, Amy reasoned. All she knew was that she didn't have time to argue with him, nor would there be ample opportunity for a lot of explanations. He looked so infuriated, and yet she was doing exactly what he wanted. She couldn't understand what was suddenly so terribly wrong.

The red flashing lights from the waiting ambulance were the first things Amy noted when they landed at Sea-Tac Airport some fifty hours later.

Amy was exhausted, emotionally and physically. The flight had been uncomfortable from the moment they'd taken off from the Kadiri Airport. Josh, although sedated, was restless and in a good deal of pain. Amy was the only one who seemed capable of calming him, so she'd stayed with him through the whole flight.

Harold Johnson was standing alongside the ambulance, looking dapper in his three-piece-suit. He hugged Amy close and assured her everything was ready and waiting for Josh at the house.

"Now what was this about me finding a nurse with the name of Brunhilde?" he asked, slipping his arm around her thin shoulders. "You were joking, weren't you? I'll have you know, Ms. Wetherell contacted five agencies, and the best we could come up with was a Bertha."

Amy chuckled, delighted that her father had taken her message so literally. "I just wanted to make sure you didn't hire someone young and pretty."

"Once you meet Mrs. White, I think you'll approve." Her father laughed with her. The worry lines around his mouth and eyes eased, and Amy realized her journey had caused him a good deal of concern, although he'd never let on. She loved him all the more for it.

"It's good to have you back, sweetheart."

"It's good to be back."

The ambulance crew were carrying Josh out of the plane on a stretcher. "Where the hell are you taking me?" he demanded.

"Josh." Amy smiled and hurried to his side. "Stop being such a poor patient."

"I'm not going back in any stuffy hospital. Understand?"

"Perfectly."

He seemed all the more flustered by her easy acquiescence. "Then where are they taking me?" His words faded as he was lifted into the interior of the ambulance.

"Home," she called after him.

"Whose home?"

The attendant closed one door at the rear of the ambulance and was reaching toward the second before Amy could respond to Josh's question.

"My home," she called after him.

"Like hell. I want a hotel room, understand? Amy, did you hear me?"

"Yes, I heard you."

The second door slammed shut. Before he could argue with her, the vehicle sped off into the night.

"It's good to be home," Amy said with an exhausted sigh. She slipped her arm around her father's trim waist and leaned her head against his strong shoulders. "By the way, that was Josh. In case you hadn't noticed, he isn't in the best of tempers. He doesn't seem to be a very good patient, but who can blame him after everything he's been through?" She lifted her gaze to her father's and sucked in a deep breath. "I almost lost him, Dad. It was so close."

"So he's being a poor patient," her father repeated, obviously trying to lighten her mood.

"Terrible. Mrs. White's going to have her hands full."

Harold Johnson took a puff of his cigar and chuckled softly. "I always hated being ordered to bed myself. I can't blame him. Fact is, I may have a good deal in common with this young man of yours."

Any smiled, realizing how true this was. "I'm sure you do. It isn't any wonder I love him so much."

Josh awoke when the golden fingers of dawn slithered through the bedroom window, creeping like a fast-growing vine over the thick oyster-gray carpet and onto the edges of his bed. Every bone in his body ached. He'd assumed that by now he would have become accustomed

to pain. He'd lived with it all these weeks, to the point
that it had almost become his friend. At least when he
was suffering, he knew he was alive. And if he was alive,
then he would be able to see Amy again.

Amy.

He shut his eyes to thoughts of her. He'd been in love
with her for months. She was warmth and sunshine, pu-
rity and generosity, and everything that was good. She
was the kind of woman a man dreams of finding—sweet
and innocent on the outside, but when he held her in his
arms, she flowered with fire and ready passion, promis-
ing him untold delights.

Yet somehow Josh was going to have to dredge up the
courage to turn his back and walk away from her.

If he was going to fall in love, he cried silently, then
why did it have to be with Harold Johnson's daughter?
The man was one of the twenty wealthiest men in the entire country. His holdings stretched from New York to
Los Angeles and several major cities in between; his name
was synonymous with achievement and high-powered
success.

Josh couldn't offer Amy this kind of life, and even if
he could, he wouldn't. He had firsthand experience of
what wealth did to a man. By age twenty-five, he had
witnessed how selfishness and greed could corrupt the
heart and tarnish the soul.

The love for money had driven a stake between Josh
and his own father, one so deep and so crippling that it
would never be healed. Eight years had passed, and not
once in all that time had Josh regretted leaving home.
Chance Powell had stared Josh in the eye and claimed he
had no son. Frankly, that information suited Josh well.
He had no father, either. He shared nothing with the man
who had sired him—nor did he wish to.

Josh's mother had died when he was in college, and his only other living relative was her sister, an elderly aunt in Boston whom he visited on rare occasions. His Aunt Hazel was getting on in years, and she seemed to make it her mission in life to try to bridge the gap between father and son, but to no avail. They were both too damn proud. Both too damn stubborn.

"I see you're awake," Bertha White, his nurse, stated as she stepped into the room. She certainly dressed for the part, donning white uniform and cap with the dedication of a conquering army.

Josh made some appropriate sound in reply. As far as he was concerned, Bertha White should be wearing a helmet with horns and singing in an opera. She marched across his room with all the grace of a herd of buffalo and pulled open the blinds, flooding the room with sunlight. Josh noted that she hadn't bothered to ask him how he felt about letting the sun blind him. Somehow he doubted that she cared.

She fussed around his bedside, apparently so he would know she was earning her salary. She checked his vital signs, dutifully entering the statistics in his chart. Then she proceeded to poke and prod him in places he didn't even want to think about. To his surprise, she graciously gave him the opportunity to wash himself.

Josh appreciated that, even if he didn't much care for the woman, who was about as warm and comforting as a mud wrestler.

"You have a visitor," she informed him once he had finished.

"Who?" Josh feared it was Amy. It would be too difficult to deal with her now, when he felt weak and vulnerable. He didn't want to hurt her, but he wasn't sure he could do what he must without causing her pain.

"Mr. Johnson is here to see you," Bertha replied stiffly, and walked out of the room.

No sooner had she departed than Amy's father let himself in, looking very much the legend Josh knew him to be. The man's presence was commanding, Josh admitted willingly. He doubted that Harold Johnson ever walked anywhere without generating a good deal of attention. Everything about him spelled prosperity and accomplishment. This one man had achieved in twenty years what three normal men couldn't do in a lifetime.

"So you're Josh Powell," Amy's father stated, his eyes as blue as his daughter's and just as kind. "I would have introduced myself when you arrived last night, but you seemed to be in a bit of discomfort."

They shook hands, and Harold casually claimed the chair at Josh's bedside, as if he often spent part of his morning visiting a sickroom.

"I'll have you know I had nothing to do with this," Josh said somewhat defiantly, wishing there was some way he could climb out of his bed and meet Johnson man-to-man.

"Nothing to do with what?"

"Being here—I had no idea Amy planned to dump me off in your backyard. Listen, I don't mean to sound like I'm ungrateful for everything you've done, but I'd like to make arrangements as soon as I can to recover elsewhere."

"Son, you're my guest."

"I would feel more comfortable someplace else," Josh insisted, gritting his teeth to a growing awareness of pain and an overabundance of pride.

"Is there a reason?" Harold didn't look unsettled by Josh's demands, only curious.

The effort to sit up was draining Josh of strength and conviction, which he struggled to disguise behind a gruff exterior. "You obviously don't know anything about me."

Harold withdrew a cigar from his inside jacket pocket and examined the end with a good deal of consideration. "My daughter certainly appears to think highly of you."

"Which doesn't say much, does it?"

"On the contrary," Harold argued. "It tells me everything I need to know."

"Then you'd better..." A sharp cramp thrust through his abdomen and he lay back and closed his eyes until it passed. "Suffice it to say, it would be best if I arranged for other accommodations. Amy should never have brought me here in the first place."

"My daughter didn't mean to offend you. In fact, I don't know if you've noticed, but she seems to have fallen head over heels in love with you."

"I noticed," Josh admitted dryly. Amy. Her name went through his mind like a hot blade. He had to leave her, couldn't her father understand that much? They were as different as the sun and the moon. As far apart as the two poles, and their dissimilarities were in ways that were impossible to bridge. Harold Johnson should be intelligent enough to recognize that with one look. Josh would have thought the man would be eager to be rid of him.

"You don't care for her?" Harold asked, chewing on the end of the cigar.

"Sir, you don't know anything about me," Josh said, taking in a calming breath. "I'm a drifter. I'm hardly suitable for your daughter. I don't want to hurt her, but I don't intend to lead her on, either."

"I see." He rubbed the side of his jaw in a thought-filled action.

It was apparent to Josh that Amy's father did nothing of the sort. "And another thing," Josh said, feeling it was important to say what was on his mind. "I can't understand how you could have let her fly to the Middle East because of me. Kadiri was no place for her."

"I agree one hundred percent. It took me an hour to come to terms with the fact she was going no matter what I said or did, so I made damn sure the road was paved for her."

"But how could you let her go and do a thing like that?" Josh demanded, still not understanding. Someone like Harold Johnson had connections, but even *his* protective arm could only stretch so far.

"I was afraid of being penalized for defensive holding," Harold said firmly.

Josh was certain he'd misunderstood. His confusion must have shown in his face, because the older man went on to explain.

"Amy's recently turned twenty-four years old and beyond the point where I can tell her what she can and can't do. If she wants to take off for the far corners of the world, there's little I can do to stop her. She knows it, and so do I. For that matter, if she's going to fall in love with you, it's not my place to tell her she's making a mistake. Either the girl's got sound judgment or she doesn't."

"I'm not good enough for her," Josh insisted.

The edges of the man's mouth lifted slightly at that. "Personally, I doubt that any man is. But I'll admit to being partial. Amy is, after all, my only child."

Josh closed his eyes, wanting to block out both the current pain and the one that was coming. If he stayed it would be inevitable. "I'm going to hurt her."

"Yes, son, I suspect you will."

"Then surely you realize why I need to get out of here, and the sooner the better."

"That's the only part I can't quite accept," Harold said slowly, his tone considerate. "As I understand it, you don't have any family close at hand?"

"None," Josh admitted reluctantly.

"Then perhaps you'd prefer several more weeks in a hospital?"

"No," Josh answered.

"Then you've made other arrangements that include a full-time nurse and—"

"No," Josh ground out harshly.

Harold Johnson's eyes filled with ill-concealed amusement.

"Your point is well taken," Josh admitted unwillingly. He didn't have a single argument that would hold up against the force of the other man's logic.

"Listen to me, son, you're welcome to remain here as long as you wish, and likewise, you're free to leave anytime you want. Neither Amy nor I would have it any other way."

"The expenses . . . ?"

"We can discuss that later," Harold told him.

"No, we'll clear the air right now. I insist upon paying for all this . . . I want that understood."

"As you wish. Now, if you'll excuse me I'd better get into the office before my secretary comes looking for me."

"Of course." Josh wanted to dislike Amy's father. It would have made life a whole lot easier. If Harold Johnson had been anything like his own father, Josh would have moved the Panama Canal to get as far away from the Johnson family as humanly possible. Instead, he'd reluctantly discovered Amy's father was the kind of man he would have gladly counted as a friend.

"Sir, I don't want you to think I don't appreciate everything you've done." Josh felt obliged to explain. "It's just that this whole setup makes me uncomfortable."

"I can't say that I blame you, boy. But you need to concentrate on getting well. You can worry about everything else later."

It commanded a good deal of effort for Josh to nod. Swirling pain wrapped its way around his body, tightening its grip on his ribs and his leg. Amy's father seemed to understand that Josh needed to rest.

"I'll be leaving you now."

"Sir." Josh half lifted his head in an effort to stop him. "If you could do one small favor for me, I'd greatly appreciate it."

"What's that?"

"Keep Amy away from me."

Harold Johnson's answering bellow of laughter was loud enough to rattle the windows. "It's obvious you don't know my daughter very well, young man. If I couldn't prevent her from flying to Timbuktu and risking her fool neck to be at your side, what makes you think I can keep her out of this sickroom?"

Josh felt an involuntary smile twitch at the corners of his mouth. Harold was right. There was nothing Josh could do to stay away from Amy. But that wasn't the worst of it. He wanted her with him, and he wasn't fooling either of them by declaring otherwise.

He must have fallen asleep, because the next thing Josh knew Bertha White was in his room, fussing around the way she had earlier in the morning. Slowly, he opened his eyes to discover the elderly woman dragging a table across the room with a luncheon tray on it.

A polite knock sounded on the door. "Ms. White."

"Yes?"

"Would it be all right if I came in now? I brought my lunch so I could eat with Josh."

"No," Josh yelled, not waiting for the other woman to answer. His nurse shot him a look that reminded him of his sixth grade teacher, who Josh swore could cuff his ears with a dirty look. "I don't feel like company," he explained.

"Come in, Miss Johnson," Mrs. White answered, daring Josh to contradict her. "I've brought the table over next to the bed so you can sit down here and enjoy your visit."

"Thank you," Amy said softly.

Josh closed his eyes. Even her voice sounded musical. Almost like an angel's. God help him; he wasn't going to be able to resist her. Not now, when he was too weak to think, much less argue.

Chapter Seven

Hi," Amy said, sitting down at the table. She carried her lunch with her—a shrimp salad and a tall glass of iced tea. Try as he might, Josh couldn't tear his eyes away from her. If her voice sounded like an angel's, it didn't even begin to compare with the way she looked. Sweet heaven, she was lovely.

"Are you feeling any better?" she asked, her eyes filled with gentle concern.

Josh thought to answer her gruffly. If he was irritable and unpleasant, then she wouldn't want to spend time with him, but one flutter of soft blue eyes and the battle was lost.

"I'm fine," he muttered, reluctantly accepting defeat. He couldn't seem to look away. She might as well have nailed him to a wall, that was how powerless he felt around her. Why did she have to be so damn sweet, so damn wonderful? Before she came to visit him, he'd tried to fortify his heart, build up his defenses. Some defenses! One look and they'd crumbled at his feet like clay.

"You're not fine," Amy countered swiftly, with a hint of indignation. "At least, that's not what I heard. Mrs. White claimed you had a restless night and have been in a good deal of pain."

"I wouldn't believe everything Robo-nurse says if I were you."

Amy chuckled, then whispered. "She is a bit intimidating, isn't she?"

"Attila the Hun incarnate."

Josh momentarily closed his eyes to enjoy the sound of her merriment as it lapped over him like a gentle wave caressing the shoreline. How he loved it when Amy laughed.

She hesitated before spreading a napkin across the lap of her jeans. "I thought it was best if we cleared the air," she said, stabbing a fat pink shrimp with her fork. She carefully avoided his gaze. "You seemed so upset with me when Dad met us at the airport the other night. I didn't mean to take charge of your life, Josh, I honestly didn't. But I suppose that's how you felt, and I certainly can't blame you." She paused long enough to chew, but while she was eating, she waved her fork around like a conductor, as if her movements would explain what she was feeling.

"Amy, I understand."

"I don't think you do," she said, once she'd swallowed. "You wanted me out of Kadiri, and I saw the perfect chance to get us *both* out, and I grabbed it. There wasn't time to consult with you about arrangements. I'm sorry if bringing you here went against your wishes. I...I did the best I could under the circumstances." She stopped long enough to suck in a giant breath. "But you're right, I should have consulted with you. I want you to know I would have, except Dr. Kilroy had heavily sedated you, and he thought it best to keep you that way for the journey. Then when we arrived everything happened so fast, and you—''

"Amy, I understand," he said quickly, interrupting her when he had the chance.

"You do?"

"Yes."

The stiffness came out of her shoulders, like air rushing from a balloon as she relaxed and reached for another shrimp. His gaze followed her action, and when she lifted the fork, she paused and smiled at him. Her happiness was contagious and free-flowing. It assailed him in a whirlwind of sensations he'd desperately struggled to repress from the moment he learned she'd flown to Kadiri to be with him.

"Want one?" she asked, her voice low and a little shaky. Her lips were moist and slightly parted as she leaned forward and held the fork in front of his mouth.

Their eyes met, and obediently he opened his mouth for her to feed him the succulent shrimp. It shouldn't have been a sensuous deed, but his heart started beating hard and strong, and the achy, restless feeling of needing to hold and kiss her fueled his mind like dry timber on a raging fire.

He longed to touch her translucent skin and plow his fingers through the silky length of her hair. But most of all, he realized, he wanted her warm and naked beneath him, making soft sounds of pleasure in his ear, and with her long, smooth legs wrapped around his waist.

His stomach knotted painfully. He leaned back and closed his eyes to the image that saturated and governed his thoughts.

She was at his side immediately, her voice filled with distress. "Should I get Mrs. White? Do you need something for the pain?"

The idea of a shot taking away the discomfort in his groin was humorous enough to curve up the edges of his mouth.

"Josh!" she blurted out. "You're smiling."

"I've got a pain, all right," he admitted, opening his eyes. He raised his hand, and trailed his fingertips across the arch of her cheek. "But it's one only you can ease."

"Tell me what to do. I want to help you. Oh, Josh, please, don't block me out. Not now, when we've been through so much together."

Gently, she planted her hands on his chest, as if that would convince him of her sincerity. Unfortunately, the action assured him of a good deal more. The ache within him intensified, and every second that she stared down on him with her bright angel eyes was adding heaps of coal to a fire that was already roaring with intensity.

"Honey, it's not that kind of pain." He wanted to shock her, awaken her to the fact they were toying with a lit fuse that was about to explode in their faces. Perhaps he was looking to frighten her a little, too, just so she would understand. Whatever his reasons, Josh firmly gripped her wrist and dragged her hand from his chest to the juncture between his legs. His eyes held hers as effectively as if she were locked within a vise, until her fingers settled over the evidence of his arousal.

Amy's eyes jolted with surprise and flickered several times as she came to terms with what lay just beneath her fingertips.

Josh, unfortunately, was in for a surprise of his own. If he'd thought his action would cure what ailed him, then he was sadly mistaken. Instead, a shaft of desire stabbed through him with such magnitude that for a wild moment it was all he could do to breathe.

Amy's hand trembled, or perhaps he was the one shivering, he couldn't tell for sure. He released her wrist, but she kept her fingers exactly where they were, tormenting him in ways she couldn't even begin to understand.

"Josh," she whispered, her voice filled with wonder and excitement. "I want you, too...there's so much for you to teach me."

Her eyes reflected the painful longing Josh was experiencing. Knowing she was feeling the same urgency only increased his desire for her. He knew he could handle his own needs, but how was he going to be able to refuse hers?

"No," he cried desperately, his control already stretched beyond endurance. The need in him felt savage, and Amy only stoked the fire by running her long nails down the length of his arousal covered by the all-too-thin sheet. The woman couldn't be *that* innocent not to realize she was driving him insane.

"Amy," he cried harshly, gripping her wrist once more. "Stop."

"It's...so hot," she whispered, her low words filled with wonder. "It makes me feel so...I don't know...so empty inside."

Josh had reached the point where reason no longer controlled him. All the arguments he'd built up against there ever being anything sexual between them vanished like mist under a noonday sun. He grasped her around the waist, half dragging her onto the bed beside him. Josh barely gave her time to adjust herself to the mattress before he kissed her, thrusting his fingers into her hair and sweeping his mouth over hers.

The kiss was hot and wild, and when her mouth opened under the force of his tongue, he rhythmically stroked hers. Amy seemed to sense that he was giving her an example of what was soon to follow, and she slid her hand over his shoulder, digging her nails into the muscles there. Her untamed response was enough to send the blood shooting through him until he thought his head would explode with it.

He found her hipbone and scooted her as close as he could, then he gloried in the way she intuitively churned the lower half of her body against him, seeking her pleasure, silently begging for the release she had yet to experience.

"Amy, help me," he groaned as he fumbled awkwardly with the buttons of her blouse. "Nourish me . . . I need you so much."

She smiled, and her whole face glowed with joy as she brushed his hands away, then expertly parted the material. Her eyes were bright with desire as she reached behind her and unclasped her bra, lowering it to expose her full breasts in a way that was so sensual he forgot to breathe. In all his experience, he'd never seen breasts like Amy's. They were full and lush, her nipples tightly beaded and pointing directly at him as if begging him to do the very thing he wanted most.

Her soft, kittenlike sound broke him from his trance and, unable to resist her a moment longer, he slid his mouth across her breasts and fastened on one taut nipple, sucking hard and strong.

Amy gave a small, startled cry, then sighed as her entire body relaxed and accepted the pleasure. Her hands were in his hair, encouraging him to take more and more of her with soft, trembling sounds that came deep from the back of her throat.

The bliss was so sharp, so keen that for Josh it reached the point of pain. The ache in his loins was unbearable. It was either take her now or stop completely.

Josh didn't have long to consider his options. His shoulders were heaving when he buried his face in the valley between her breasts, rubbing his mouth back and forth in sharp denial. It took him several seconds to compose himself, and even then he felt as shaky as a tree limb caught in a hurricane.

"Josh?" Amy's voice was filled with question. "What's wrong?"

Slowly, he lifted his head, struggling to maintain the last fragment of his control before it snapped completely. Gently, he kissed her lips, while he awkwardly attempted to refasten her blouse.

"Did I hurt you?" she asked, her voice low and warm, throbbing with concern.

Her question tugged at his heart with powerful threads, affecting Josh more than any in his life. He'd come within a hair's space of making love with her, driven to the edge of insanity by need and desire. His burning passion had dominated his every move. He might have frightened her, or worse, hurt her. The hot ache in him had been too strong to have taken the proper amount of care to be sure this first time was right. And Amy was concerned that she'd hurt *him*.

"Josh?" She repeated her question with his name, grazing his face with gentle, caressing fingers.

"I'm fine. Did I hurt you?"

"No...never. It was wonderful, but why did you stop?"

"Remember Robo-nurse?"

It was obvious that Amy had completely forgotten Bertha White by the startled look that flashed into her soft blue eyes. "Did she . . . is she back?"

"No, but she will be soon enough." Bertha was an excuse, Josh realized, a valid one, but she wasn't the reason he'd pulled away. He'd been about to lose all control, and God help him, he couldn't allow that to happen.

For two frustrating days, Amy's visits to Josh were limited to short ten-minute stays. Her father had her running errands for him. The charity bazaar she had worked on earlier that summer needed her for another project, and then Manuela had taken sick.

Everything seemed to be working against her being with Josh. It seemed every time she came, wanting to be alone with Josh, his nurse found an excuse to linger there. Amy wondered if he had put the older woman up to it. That was a silly thought, she realized, because he didn't seem to be any more fond of Bertha than Amy was.

Her thoughts were abuzz with questions. Every time her mind focused on the things Josh had done to her, the way he had feasted on her breasts, she grew warm and achy inside. The pleasure had been like nothing she had ever known, and once sampled, it created a need for more. She felt as though she had stood at the precipice, seeking something she couldn't name. Now that she had gazed upon such uncharted territory she was lost, filled with questions with no one to answer them.

It was late and dark and her father had retired for the evening. Amy lay in bed, restlessly trying to concentrate on a novel. The effort was useless, and she knew it. Every thought that entered her head had to do with Josh.

Throwing aside the sheets, she reached for her satin robe and searched out her slippers, which were hiding beneath her bed. Never in all her life had she done anything so bold as what she was about to do now.

She paused outside her bedroom door in the softly lit hallway and waited for reason to lead her back where she belonged. Nothing drove her backward. Instead she felt compelled to move forward.

Thankfully, at this time of night Bertha White would be sound asleep. As silently as possible Amy closed the door, then proceeded down the wide hallway to Josh's room.

The first thing she noticed was that his reading light was on. The sight relaxed her. She hadn't looked forward to waking him.

"Hello, Josh," she said as she silently stepped into the room. She closed the door, and when she turned around, she noticed that he was sitting up, gazing at her with dark, intense eyes.

"It's late," he announced starkly.

"Yes, I know. I couldn't sleep."

He eyed her wearily. "I was just about to turn out my light."

"I won't be a minute. It's just that I have a few questions for you, and I realize this is probably pretty embarrassing, but there isn't anyone else I can ask."

He closed his book, but she noticed that he didn't set it aside. In fact, he was holding it as if the hardbound novel would be enough of a barrier to keep her away.

"Questions about what?"

"The other day when we—"

"Damn it, Amy, that was a mistake."

She blinked back the hurt and swallowed tightly before continuing. "I don't know why you say that. Every time you so much as touch me, you claim it was a mistake. It's damn frustrating."

A hint of a smile bounced against his eyes and mouth. "What do you want to know?" he asked, not unkindly. "And I'll do my level best to answer you."

"Without making a comment about the rightness or wrongness of what's happening between us?"

"All right," he agreed.

"Thank you." She pulled up a chair and sat, her gaze level with his own. Now that she had his full attention, she wasn't sure exactly where to start. Twice she opened her mouth, only to abruptly close it again, her muddled thoughts stumbling over themselves.

"I'm waiting," he said with a dash of impatience.

"Yes, well, this isn't exactly easy." She could feel a blush work its way up her face, and was confident she was about to make a complete idiot of herself. Briefly Amy had thought that if her mother had been alive, she could have asked her, but on second thought, she realized this was something one didn't discuss with one's mother.

"Amy," he questioned softly, "what is it?"

Her gaze was lowered, and the heat creeping up from her neck had blossomed into full color in her cheeks. She absently toyed with the satin ties at the neck of her robe.

"I . . . when we—you know—were on the bed together, you said something that has been on my mind ever since."

"What did I say?"

Josh sounded so calm, so...ordinary, as if he had this type of discussion with women every day of the week, as if he were a doctor discussing a medical procedure with his patient. Amy's heart was thundering in her ears so loudly she could barely form a coherent thought.

He prompted her again, and she wound the satin tie around her index finger so tightly she cut off the circulation. "You were trying to undo my blouse," she whispered, nearly choking on the words.

"And?"

"And you asked me to nourish you, and I did ... at least I think I did."

"Yes, you most certainly did."

Just talking about it made her nipples begin to tingle again, the way they had when his mouth had been over them. It was all Amy could do not to cover her face and flee.

"It felt so good."

"It did for me, too." Josh's voice was low and hesitant.

"Will you do it again?" she asked, her voice so quiet she could barely hear herself. "Will you let me nourish you again?" Boldly she raised her eyes to his, her heart beating wildly.

She stood and walked the few short steps to his bedside and laid open her robe. Josh sat there mesmerized, his face unreadable, but he didn't say or do anything to stop her. Her fingers were trembling as she slipped the robe from her shoulders. It fell silently at her feet, and she focused her concentration on the buttons of her silk pajama tops, exposing her breasts to him, making herself vulnerable in ways she was only beginning to comprehend. She was so pale, she realized, wishing now that she was tan and golden for him, instead of alabaster white.

"Amy."

Her name was little more than a rasp between his lips. "You don't know what you're asking." Of their own volition, it seemed, his fingers lightly brushed the smooth skin of her breasts. Instantly, her nipples puckered and began throbbing.

His touch, although feather-light, produced an immediate melting ache between her legs. She pulsed in places she'd never known existed until Josh had kissed and touched her. He rotated his thumb over the hardened peak, and a whimper escaped before she could swallow the needy cry. Although the sound was barely audible, it seemed to vibrate all across the room, bouncing back to her like a sonic boom.

"Please, Josh," she whispered. "I have to know." There was more she longed to ask, more she yearned to discover, but the words withered on the end of her tongue at the look of intense longing Josh gave her.

He reached for her waist and gently urged her forward until she was close enough for him to bury his face between her breasts. His open mouth blazed a moist trail between the two, sucking from each, sampling and tasting until Amy thought she was going to lose her mind.

Closing her eyes to the mounting delight, she tossed her head back and reveled in the hungry suckling. She gasped, hardly able to bear the hot flood of pleasure that shot from her breast to the apex of her womanhood.

It wasn't just her breasts that tingled now, but her entire body. Her own flesh was alien to her, and she didn't know what to expect or how she was supposed to react.

Abruptly, Josh stopped and jerked his head away. For several seconds he did nothing but draw in deep, lung-rasping breaths. "There," he said finally. "Does that answer your question?"

Amy clung to him, not knowing how to tell him that he hadn't answered a single inquiry. Instead he'd created even more.

"I don't want you to stop," she moaned in bewilderment. She paused, hoping to clear her thoughts, then continued raggedly. "Josh, I want to make love with you. I want you to teach me to be a woman, your woman."

"No."

Her knees would no longer support her, and she sank onto the bed, sitting on the edge of the mattress. It was then that she realized that Josh was trembling, and the knowledge that she could make him want her so desperately filled her with a heady sense of power.

Barely recognizing what she was doing, Amy pressed him back against the mattress and lifted both legs onto the bed, straddling him carefully. Wordlessly, she lowered her mouth and outlined his lips with the tip of her tongue, teasing him, taunting him, stroking his tongue with her own, imitating the things he'd done with her when he'd gathered her in his arms upon this very mattress. She nipped at his lower lip, then found his earlobe and sucked at it as greedily and hungrily as he had on her breasts.

"No," he cried a second time, but with much less conviction. Even as he spoke he filled his palms with her breasts and made a low, rough sound of protest. "Amy...please." His voice vibrated between them, filled with urgency and helplessness. "Not like this...not in your father's house."

She sagged, drooping her head in frustration. Josh was right. They were both panting with the effort to resist each other as it was, and in a few seconds neither one of them would be able to stop. It took everything within her to quit now.

Climbing off the bed, she blindly reached for her pajama top and her robe. She would have turned and vaulted from the room if Josh hadn't reached for her wrist, stalling her. Not for anything could she look him in the eye.

"Are you going to be all right?" he asked.

She nodded wildly, knowing it was a lie. She would never be the same again.

He swore quietly, and with a muffled deep gasp of pain sat upright in the bed and reached for her, hugging her close and burying his face in the gentle slope of her neck.

"Dear God, Amy, we've got to stop this horsing around before it kills the both of us."

"Josh," she whispered, her tone hesitant. "That's the problem. I don't want to stop. It feels so wonderful when you touch me, and I get all achy inside and out." Consternation and apprehension crept into her voice. "This is embarrassing the hell out of you, isn't it?"

"Me?"

"I mean, the last thing you need is me making all kinds of sexual demands on you. Dear heaven, you're lucky to be alive. Here I am, like a kid who's recently discovered a wonderful toy and doesn't quite know how to make everything work."

"Believe me, honey, it's working."

"I'm sorry, Josh, I really am—"

He silenced her with a chaste kiss. "Go back to bed. We can talk more about it in the morning, when both our heads are clear."

"Good night," she whispered, heaving a sigh.

"Good night." He kissed her once more and, with a reluctance that tore at her heart, he released her.

"Morning, Dad," Amy said as she seated herself at the table for breakfast the following morning.

Her father grumbled an inaudible reply, which wasn't anything like him. Harold Johnson had always been a morning person and boomed enthusiasm for each new day.

Amy hesitated, her thoughts in a whirl. Was it possible that her father had heard her sneak into Josh's room the night before? That thought was enough to produce a heated blush, and in an effort to disguise her discomfort, she hurriedly dished up her scrambled eggs and bacon.

Her father didn't say anything more for several minutes. Deciding it would be better to confront him with the truth than suffer this intolerable silence, Amy straightened her shoulders and clasped her hands in her lap.

"How's Josh doing?" Harold asked, reaching for the sugar bowl after pouring himself a cup of coffee.

"Better." She eyed him warily, trying to decide the best way to handle this awkward situation. Perhaps she should let him bring up the subject first.

"I talked to Mrs. White yesterday afternoon," she said with feigned cheerfulness, "and she said Josh is doing better than anyone expected."

"Good. Good."

Enthusiasm echoed in each word. Amy was absolutely positive that her father knew the reasons behind Josh's increasing strength. The crimson heat that had invaded her face earlier circled her ears like a lariat. She swallowed a bite of her toast, and it settled in her stomach like a lead ball.

"I had a chance to talk to Mrs. White this morning myself."

"You did?" she blurted out.

"Yes," he continued, eyeing her closely.

Amy did her level best to disguise her distress. She'd always been close to her father, and other than the business about him making her a part of Johnson Industries, she'd prided herself on being able to talk to him about anything.

"Amy, are you feeling all right?"

"Sure, Dad," she said energetically, knowing she wasn't going to be able to fool him.

He arched his brows and reached for his coffee, sipping at it while he continued studying her.

There was nothing left to do but blurt out the truth and clear the air before she suffocated in the tension. "You heard me last night, didn't you?"

"I beg your pardon?"

"Well, you needn't concern yourself, because nothing happened. Well, almost nothing, but not from lack of trying on my part. Josh was the perfect gentleman."

Her father stared at her with huge blue eyes. He certainly wasn't making this any easier on her. He continued to glare at her for several uneasy seconds until Amy felt compelled to explain further.

"It was late . . . and I couldn't sleep. I know that probably isn't a very good excuse, but I had a question that I wanted to ask Josh."

"You couldn't have asked me?"

Her startled eyes flew to him. "No!"

"Go on."

"What more do you want to know? I already told you nothing happened."

"I believe the phrase you used a moment ago was 'almost nothing.'"

"I'm crazy about him, Dad, and I've never been in love before, and, well, it's damn difficult when you . . . feel that way about someone . . . if you know what I mean?"

"I believe I do."

"Good." She relaxed somewhat. Although her appetite had vanished the instant she realized her father was waiting to confront her about what had happened in

Josh's room, she did an admirable job of finishing her breakfast.

"Mrs. White said Josh would be able to join us for dinner tonight."

Amy's happy gaze flew to her father. "That's wonderful."

"I thought you'd be pleased to hear it."

"I'll have Manuela prepare a special dinner."

Her father nodded. "Good idea." He downed the last of his coffee, glanced at his watch, then stood abruptly. "I've got to go to the office. Have a good day, sweetheart."

Amy raised her coffee cup to her lips and sipped. "Thanks. You, too."

"I will." He was halfway out of the dining room when he turned around. "Amy."

"Yes, Dad."

"I'm not exactly certain I should admit this. But I didn't hear a damn thing last night. I slept like a log."

Chapter Eight

It's your move," Amy reminded Josh for the second time, growing restless. Just how long did it take to move a silly chess piece, anyway?

Josh nodded, frowning slightly as he studied the board that rested on the table between them.

Amy's gaze caught her father's and she rolled her eyes. Josh was the one who'd insisted they play chess following dinner. Harold Johnson shared a secret smile with her. He pretended to be reading when in fact he was closely watching their game.

Amy had never been much of a chess player; she didn't have the patience for it. As far as she was concerned, chess was a more difficult version of checkers, and she chose to play it that way. It never took her more than a few seconds to move her pieces. Josh, on the other hand, drove her crazy, analyzing each move she made, trying to figure out her strategy. Heaven knew she didn't have one, and no one was more shocked than she was when Josh announced that she'd placed him in checkmate. Good grief, she hadn't even noticed.

"You're an excellent player," he said, leaning back and rubbing the side of his jaw. He continued to study the board as though he couldn't quite figure out how she'd done it. Amy hoped he would let her in on the secret once he figured it out; she was curious to find out herself.

Her father rose from his wingback leather chair and crossed the room to get a book from the mahogany cases that lined two walls. As soon as he was out of earshot, Amy glanced over to Josh.

"You haven't kissed me all week," she whispered heatedly.

Josh's anxious gaze flew to her father, then to her. "I don't plan to."

"Ever again?"

Josh frowned. "Not here."

"Why not?"

"Because! Damn it, Amy, can't we discuss this another time?"

"No," she answered with equal fervor. "You're driving me crazy."

"Mr. Johnson," Josh said anxiously and cleared his throat when her father started toward his chair. "Could I interest you in a game of chess?"

"No thanks, son. Amy's the champion of our family, you're going to have to demand a rematch with her." He stopped and placed his hand over his mouth, then did a poor job of feigning a yawn. "The fact is, I was thinking of heading up to bed. I seem to be tired this evening."

"It's barely eight," Amy protested. She immediately regretted her outburst. With her father safely tucked away in his bedroom, she might be able to spend a few minutes alone with Josh, which was something she hadn't been able to do in days.

"Can't help it if I'm tired," Harold grumbled and, after bidding them both good night, he walked out of the room.

Amy waited a few moments until she was sure her father was completely up the stairs. "All right, Joshua Powell, kindly explain yourself."

"The subject's closed, Amy."

She bolted to her feet, her fists digging into her hipbones as she struggled to quell her irritation. "Subject? What subject?"

"You and me . . . kissing."

If his face hadn't been so twisted with consternation and pride, she would have laughed outright. Unfortunately, Josh was dead serious.

"You don't want to kiss me anymore? At all?"

He tossed her a look that told her she should know otherwise by now. Reaching for his crutches, he struggled to his feet. The cast had been removed from his leg, but he still had trouble walking without support.

"Where are you going?" she demanded, growing more agitated by the minute.

"To bed."

"Oh, honestly," she cried. "There's no reason to wrestle your way up those stairs so early. If you're so desperate to escape me, then I'll leave."

"Amy . . ."

"No." She stopped him by holding up both hands. "There's no need to worry your stubborn little head about me taking a drive alone in the cold, dark city. There are plenty of places I can go, so sit down and enjoy yourself. You must be sick of that room upstairs."

SILHOUETTE GIVES YOU SIX REASONS TO CELEBRATE!

MAIL THE BALLOON TODAY!

INCLUDING:

**1.
4 FREE
BOOKS**

**2.
A LOVELY 20k GOLD
ELECTROPLATED CHAIN**

**3.
A SURPRISE
BONUS**

AND MORE!

TAKE A LOOK...

Yes, become a Silhouette subscriber and the celebration goes on forever.

To begin with we'll send you:

4 new Silhouette Special Edition® novels — FREE

a lovely 20k gold electroplated chain—FREE

an exciting mystery bonus—FREE

And that's not all! Special extras— Three more reasons to celebrate.

4. FREE Home Delivery! That's right! We'll send you 4 FREE books, and you'll be under no obligation to purchase any in the future. You may keep the books and return the accompanying statement marked cancel.

If we don't hear from you, about a month later we'll send you six additional novels to read and enjoy. If you decide to keep them, you'll pay the low members only discount price of just $2.74* each — that's 21 cents less than the cover price — AND there's **no** extra charge for delivery! There are **no** hidden extras! **You may cancel at any time!** But as long as you wish to continue, every month we'll send you six more books, which you can purchase or return at our cost, cancelling your subscription.

5. Free Monthly Newsletter! It's the indispensable insiders' look at our most popular writers and their upcoming novels. Now you can have a behind-the-scenes look at the fascinating world of Silhouette! It's an added bonus you'll look forward to every month!

6. More Surprise Gifts! Because our home subscribers are our most valued readers, we'll be sending you additional free gifts from time to time — as a token of our appreciation.

*Terms and prices subject to change without notice.
Sales tax applicable in NY and Iowa. © 1989 Harlequin Enterprises Ltd.

FREE! 20k GOLD ELECTROPLATED CHAIN!

You'll love this 20k gold electroplated chain! The necklace is finely crafted with 160 double-soldered links, and is electroplate finished in genuine 20k gold. It's nearly 1/8" wide, fully 20" long — and has the look and feel of the real thing. "Glamorous" is the perfect word for it, and it can be yours FREE in this amazing Silhouette celebration!

SILHOUETTE SPECIAL EDITION®

FREE OFFER CARD

4 FREE BOOKS

20k GOLD ELECTROPLATED CHAIN—FREE

FREE MYSTERY BONUS

PLACE YOUR BALLOON STICKER HERE!

FREE HOME DELIVERY

FREE FACT-FILLED NEWSLETTER

MORE SURPRISE GIFTS THROUGHOUT THE YEAR—FREE

YES! Please send me my four Silhouette Special Edition® novels FREE, along with my 20k Electroplated Gold Chain and my free mystery gift, as explained on the opposite page. I understand that accepting these books and gifts places me under no obligation ever to buy any books. I may cancel at any time for any reason, and the free books and gifts will be mine to keep!   235 CIS RIYJ (U-S-SE-02/90)

NAME _____
(PLEASE PRINT)

ADDRESS _____ APT _____

CITY _____ STATE _____

ZIP _____

Offer limited to one per household and not valid to current Silhouette Special Edition subscribers. Terms and prices subject to change without notice. All orders subject to approval.

© 1989 HARLEQUIN ENTERPRISES LTD.

SILHOUETTE "NO RISK GUARANTEE"
• There's no obligation to buy — the free books and gifts remain yours to keep.
• You receive books before they're available in stores.
• You may end your subscription anytime — just by letting us know.

PRINTED IN U.S.A

Remember! To receive your free books, chain and a surprise
mystery bonus, return the postpaid card below.
But don't delay.

DETACH AND MAIL CARD TODAY
If offer card has been removed, write to: Silhouette Reader Service,
901 Fuhrmann Blvd., P.O. Box 1867, Buffalo, NY 14269-1867

FILL OUT THIS POSTPAID CARD AND MAIL TODAY!

BUSINESS REPLY CARD
FIRST CLASS   PERMIT NO. 717   BUFFALO, N.Y.

Postage will be paid by addressee

SILHOUETTE BOOKS®

901 Fuhrmann Blvd.,
P.O. Box 1867
Buffalo, N.Y. 14240-9952

NO POSTAGE
NECESSARY
IF MAILED
IN THE
UNITED STATES

With a proud thrust of her chin she marched out of the room and retrieved her purse. Glancing over her shoulder, she sighed and added, "There's no need to fret. Seattle has one of the lowest murder rates on the west coast." She had no idea if this was true or not, but it sounded good.

"Amy," he shouted, and followed her. His legs swung wide as he maneuvered his crutches around the corner of the hallway, nearly colliding with her.

She offered him a brave smile and pretended she wasn't the least bit disturbed by his attitude, when exactly the opposite was true. If he didn't want to kiss or hold her again then . . . then she would just have to accept it.

"Yes?" she asked, tightly clenching the car keys in her hand as though keeping them safely tucked between her fingers was the most important thing in her life.

For a long moment Josh did nothing but stare at her. A battle raged in his expression as if he was fighting himself. Whichever side won apparently didn't please him, because his shoulders sagged and he slowly shook his head. "Do you want company?"

"Are you suggesting you come along with me?"

His smile was off center. "What do you think?"

"I don't know anymore, Josh. You haven't been yourself all week. Do you think I'm so blind I haven't noticed how you've arranged it so we're never alone together anymore?"

"It's too much temptation," he argued heatedly. "We're in trouble here, Amy. We're so hot for each other it's a minor miracle that we don't burst into spontaneous combustion every time we touch."

"So you're making sure that doesn't happen again?"

"You're damn right," he returned forcefully. He was leaning heavily upon his crutches. He wiped a hand over his face as if to erase her image from his mind. "I don't like it any better than you do, Angel Eyes."

Somehow Amy doubted that. Her tight look must have said as much because Josh emitted a harsh groan.

"Do you have any idea how much I want to make love with you?" he asked her in a harsh whisper. "Every time you walk into the room, it's pure torment. Tonight at dinner, I swear I didn't take my eyes off your breasts the entire meal. Dear God, how do you make them pucker and point at me like that?"

She smiled, not knowing how to answer him.

"Then you got up and walked away, and it was all I could do to keep from watching your sweet little tush swaying back and forth. I kept thinking how good it would be to place my hands there and cuddle you against me. Did you honestly believe I wanted seconds of dessert? The fact was, I didn't dare stand up."

"Oh, Josh." Her smile was watery with relief.

He held open his arms for her, and she walked into them the way a frightened child ducks into a family home, sensing security and safety. His legs were braced apart, and he nestled her between them, the hard proof of his arousal evident, pressing against her abdomen. Using the wall to brace his shoulders, he set one crutch aside and reached for her, wrapping his arm around her waist. Slowly, he lowered his hand, lifting her toward him so he could press himself more intimately against her. His eyes drifted shut as he groaned from between clenched teeth.

"Josh . . ."

"Do you understand now?" he ground out, close to her ear.

"Yes," she whispered with a barely audible release of breath. She slipped her arms around his neck and nodded, gyrating her hips as the first twinge of excitement shot through her blood.

He stroked his thumb along the side of her neck and inhaled a wobbly breath before he spoke again. "Now, what was it you were saying about going for a ride?"

"Ride?" she repeated in a daze.

"Yes, Amy, a ride, as in a motorized vehicle, preferably with all the windows down and the air conditioner on full blast so my blood will cool."

She pressed her forehead to his chin and smiled before reluctantly breaking away from him. Josh reached for his crutch and followed her through the kitchen and to the garage just beyond.

A few minutes later, with Amy driving and Josh sitting in the passenger seat, they headed down the long, curved driveway and onto the street, turning east toward Lake Washington.

"I love Seattle at night," Amy said, smiling at him. "There're so many bright lights, and the view of the water is fantastic."

"Where are you taking me?"

"Lover's Leap?" she teased.

"Try again."

"All right, it isn't exactly Lover's Leap, but it is a viewpoint that looks out onto the lake. It's been a while since I've been there, but from what I remember, it's worth the drive."

"And what exactly do you know about lookout points, Amy Johnson? I'd bet my entire life's savings that you've never been there with a man."

"Then you'd lose." She tossed him a saucy grin, then pulled her gaze to the roadway, her love for him so potent she felt giddy with it.

He eyed her skeptically. "Who?"

"Does it matter? All you need to know is that I was there with a man. A handsome one, too, by anyone's standards."

"When?" he challenged.

"Well," she hesitated, not wanting to give her secret away quite so easily. "I don't exactly remember *when*. Let me suffice to say, it was several years back, when I was young and foolish."

"You're young and foolish now."

"Nevertheless, I was with a man. I believe you said you'd hand over your life savings to me." She laughed, her happiness bubbling over. "I'll take a check, but only with the proper identification."

"All right, if you're going to make this difficult, I'll guess. You were ten and your daddy was escorting you around town and stopped at this lookout point so you could view the city lights."

"How'd you guess that?" she asked, then clamped her mouth shut, realizing she'd given herself away. "I should make you pay for that, Joshua Powell."

He brushed his fingers against her nape, and when he spoke his voice was low and seductive. "I'm counting on it, Angel Eyes."

"You think once I park this car that I'm going to let you kiss me, don't you?"

Josh's laugh was full. "Baby, you're going to ask for it. Real nice, too."

Laughing, she eased the Mercedes to a stop at the end of the long, deserted street and turned off the headlights, then the ignition. The view was as magnificent as she remembered. More so, because she was sharing it with Josh. The city stretched out before them like a bolt of black satin, littered with shimmering lights that sparkled and gleamed like diamonds. Lake Washington was

barely visible, but the electricity from the homes that
bordered its shores traced the curling banks. The sky was
cloudless and the moon full.

Amy expelled her breath and leaned her head back to
gaze into the heavens. It was so peaceful, so quiet, the
moment serene. It was a small wonder that this area
hadn't been developed over the intervening years since
she'd last been here. She was pleased that it remained
unspoiled, because it would have ruined everything to
have this lovely panorama defaced with long rows of expensive homes.

Josh was silent, apparently savoring the sight himself.

"All right," she whispered, her voice trembling a little with anticipation.

He turned to her, his mending leg stretched out in front
of him in as comfortable a position the cramped quarters of the car could afford him. The crutches were bal-
anced against the passenger door. "All right what?"

"You said I was going to have to ask for a kiss. I'm
asking, Josh." She felt breathless, as if she'd just finished playing a set of tennis. "Please."

Josh went stock-still, and she could sense the tension
in him as strongly as she could smell the fragrant grass
that grew along the roadside.

"God help me, Amy, I want to please you."

"You do, every time we touch."

He turned her in his arms, his kiss slow and sultry. So
hot and sweet that her toes curled and she twisted, wanting to get as near to him as possible in the close con-
fines. The console was a barrier between them, and the
steering wheel prevented her from twisting more than just
a little.

In their weeks together, Josh had taught her the fine art
of kissing, his lessons exhaustive and detailed. Tonight,

Amy was determined to prove to him what an avid student she had been. She welcomed his tongue and teased him with her own, stroking the inside of his mouth until he groaned and abruptly broke off the kiss. His shoulders heaved, and he drew in a sharp breath.

"Amy," he warned in a severe whisper, "you should never have gotten us started. Angel, don't you understand yet what this is eventually going to lead to—"

She pressed the tips of her fingers over his lips. "Why do you insist on arguing with me, Joshua Powell?" She didn't give him an opportunity to answer, but slid her hands up his shoulders and joined them at the base of his neck, lifting her mouth to his once more, unwilling to spend these precious moments alone debating a moot point.

Josh's kiss wasn't slow or sweet this time, but hot and urgent, so hungry that he drove the crown of her head against the headrest. He grasped the material of her skirt, bunching it up around her upper thighs as he slid his callused palm over her silk panties.

Her eyes snapped open with surprise at this new invasion. He wanted to shock her, prove to her that she was in over her head. What Josh didn't realize was that with all the other lessons he'd been giving her, she'd learned to swim. So well she wanted to try out for the Olympic team. Lifting her hips just a little to aid him, her knee came in sharp contact with the steering wheel, and she cried out softly.

"Damn."

"If you think that's bad, I've got a gear shift sticking in my ribs," he informed her between nibbling kisses. "I'm too old for this, Angel Eyes."

"I am, too," she whispered and teased him with her tongue.

"Maybe I'm not as old as I think," he amended at the end of a ragged sigh.

Amy smoothed the hair away from his face, spreading eager kisses wherever she could. "You know what I want?"

"Probably the same thing I do, but we aren't going to get it in this car."

"Honestly, Josh, you've got a one-track mind."

"Me!" he bellowed, then groaned and broke away from her to rub the ache from his right leg.

"Are you all right?" Amy asked, unable to bear the thought of Josh in pain.

"Let me put it this way," he said, a frown pleating his brow. "I don't want you to kiss it and make it better."

"Why not?" She tried to sound as offended as she felt.

"Because the ache in my leg is less than the one that console is giving my ribs. If this is to go any farther, then it won't be in this car."

"Agreed." Without another word, she snapped her seat belt into place, turned on the ignition and shifted the gears into reverse. Her tires kicked up loose gravel and dirt as she backed into the street.

"*Now* where are you taking me?" Josh asked, chuckling.

"Don't ask."

"I was afraid of that," he muttered.

A half hour later, they turned off the road onto the driveway that led to her family home. She drove past the garage and the tennis courts and parked directly in front of the pool.

"What are we doing here?" he demanded, looking none too pleased.

"I tried to say something earlier," she reminded him, "but you kept interrupting me. I think we should go swimming."

He groaned and shut his eyes, obviously less than enthusiastic with her suggestion. "Swimming? In case you hadn't noticed it's October, and there's a definite nip in the air."

"The pool's heated. Eighty-two degrees, to be exact."

"I don't have a suit."

"There are several your size in the cabana."

Josh closed his fingers around the door handle. Slowly shaking his head, he opened the door and, using both hands, carefully swung out his right leg. "I have the distinct notion you have an argument for every one of my objections."

"I do." She climbed out of the car, and with her arm around his waist, she guided him toward the changing room and brought out several suits for him to choose from. She kissed him, then smiled at him. "The last one in the water is a rotten egg."

By the time Amy came out of the cabana, Josh was sitting at the deep end, his long legs dangling in the pool. He was right about there being a chill in the night air. She kept the thick towel securely wrapped around her shoulders as she walked over to join him, but she did this more for effect than to ward off the cold.

"Hello, rotten egg."

"Hi, there," she said, giving him a slow, sweet smile before letting the towel drop to her feet.

The minute she did, Josh gasped and his eyes seemed to pop out of their sockets. "Oh, God," he muttered.

"Do you like it?" she asked, whirling around in a wide circle for him to admire her itsy-bitsy string bikini.

"You mean, do I like what there is of it?"

She smiled, pleased to the soles of her feet by his response. "I picked it up in France last summer. Trust me, this one is modest compared to what some of the other women were wearing."

"Or not wearing," he commented dryly. "You'd be arrested if you showed up in that...thing on any beaches around here."

Holding her head high to appear as statuesque as possible, she smiled softly, turned and dipped her big toe into the pool to test the temperature. "I most certainly would *not* be arrested. Admired, perhaps, but not imprisoned."

His Adam's apple moved up and down his throat, but he didn't take his eyes off her. "Have you...worn this particular suit often?"

"No. There was never anyone I wanted to see me in it until now." With that, she stood at the edge of the pool, raised her arms high above her head and dove headlong into the turquoise blue waters, slicing the surface with her slender frame.

She surfaced, sputtering and angry. "Damn. Oh, double damn."

"What's wrong?"

"You don't want to know." Before he could question her further, she dove under the clear blue water and held her breath for as long as she could.

When she broke the surface, gasping for breath, Josh was in the pool beside her, treading water. He took one look at her and started to laugh.

"You lost your fancy bikini top," he cried, as if she hadn't noticed.

"I suppose you find this all very amusing," she said, blushing to the roots of her hair. To her horror, she discovered that women's breasts have the uncanny habit of floating. Trying to maintain as much dignity as possible, she pressed her splayed fingers over her lush breasts, flattening them to her torso. But she soon discovered that without her hands, she couldn't stay afloat. Her lips went below the waterline, and she drank in several mouthfuls before choking. Mortified, she abandoned the effort, deciding it was better to be immodest than to drown.

Josh was laughing, and it was all she could do not to dunk him. "The least you can do is try to help me find it."

"Not on your life. Fact is, this unfortunate incident is going to save me a good deal of time and trouble."

"Josh." She held out her hand. "I insist that you . . . keep your distance." She eyed him warily while clumsily working her way toward the shallow end of the pool.

"Look at that," he said, his gaze centering on her breasts, which were bobbing up and down at the surface as she tried to get away from him. "Even now they insist on pointing at me."

Her toes scraped the bottom of the pool, and once her feet were secure, she scrunched down, keeping just her head visible. She covered her face with both hands. "This is downright embarrassing, and all you can do is laugh."

"I'm sorry."

But he didn't sound the least bit petulant.

"I wanted you to see me in that bikini and swoon with desire. You were supposed to take one look at me and be so overcome with passion that you could hardly speak."

"I was."

"No, you weren't," she challenged. "In fact you looked angry, telling me I should be arrested."

"I didn't say that exactly."

"Close enough," she cried, her discontent gaining momentum. "I spent an extra ten minutes in the cabana spreading baby oil all over my body so I'd glisten for you, and did you notice? Oh, no, you—"

Before another word passed her lips, Josh had gripped her by the waist and carried her to the corner of the pool, securing her there and blocking any means of escape with his body. His outstretched arms gripped the edge of the pool.

Wide-eyed, she stared at him, the only light coming from the full moon and the dim blue lights below the water. Her lashes were wet with tears and she bit into her lower lip, feeling like a fool.

"It isn't any big disaster," Josh told her.

"Oh, sure, you're not the one floating around with your private parts exposed. Trust me, it has a humbling effect."

She knew he was trying not to laugh, but it didn't help matters when the corners of his mouth started quivering. "Joshua Powell," she cried, bracing her hands against his shoulders and pushing for all she was worth. "I could just—"

"Kiss me." The teasing light had vanished and he lowered his gaze to the waterline. His eyes were dark and narrowed, and her breasts felt heavy and swollen just from the way he was looking at her.

Timidly, she slanted her mouth over his, barely brushing his lips with her own.

"Not like that," he protested, threading his fingers through her wet, blond hair. "Kiss me the way you did earlier in the car." His voice was low and velvety. "Oh, baby," he moaned, slipping his moist mouth back and forth over her own. "The things you do to me." Seemingly impatient, he took advantage of her parted lips, probing inside with his tongue, his investigation thorough and leisurely. He was kissing her as he never had before, tasting, relishing, savoring her in a hungry exchange that left them both breathless.

"Wrap your legs around my waist," he instructed, his words raspy with desire.

Without question she did as he asked. Slipping her hands over the smooth-powered muscles, she gloried in his arousal.

"Josh?"

"Yes, love."

She didn't know what she wanted to ask, only that there was this incredible heaviness in the lower part of her body that only a moment before had been throbbing in her breasts. The feeling was growing more intense.

She slipped her arms around his neck and pressed her nipples against the water-slickened planes of his chest, rotating her torso back and forth to ease the tension, and instead sparking an exciting new friction.

"Are you...hungry?" she asked, her voice little more than a husky murmur.

His response was guttural. "You know that I am."

"And I know how...to nourish you." With her palms braced against his shoulders, she levered herself out of the water just far enough to offer him her breasts. His mouth latched on to her nipple, sucking voraciously yet gently, plunging her into a wild mingling of pleasures she had never experienced. Hot, burning sensation sang along the ends of her nerves until Amy was convinced they were about to overload. Moaning, she thrashed her hips against him.

"Angel," he whimpered, "be still for just a moment."

"I can't," she cried breathlessly.

Somehow Josh was able to untie the strings that held together the bottom half of her bikini. Then slowly, gradually, he lowered his hand toward the area that had become the pulsating center of her being. He reached for her, seeking to take intimate possession of her, exploring the innermost part of her body. As he slipped his finger inside her, Amy threw back her head, barely able to catch her breath. Her shoulders started shaking as a soft, mewling sound rose deep from within her throat.

Her nails curled into his chest, but if the action caused him any pain, he gave no indication. The need to taste him dominated every thought as she ran the tip of her tongue around the circumference of his mouth. His tongue joined hers until the pulsating climax rocked through her, sending out rippling waves of release.

Her breasts were heaving when she collapsed on him. "Oh, Josh, I never knew...I never knew." She was just regaining her breath when she heard the sound of voices and laughter advancing from the other side of the cabana.

Josh heard it as well and stiffened, tension filling his body. "Who's there?" he shouted, his body shielding Amy from view.

"Peter Stokes."

Josh's questioning gaze met Amy's. "He's our gardener's son," she explained in a whisper. "Dad told him he could come swimming anytime...but not now."

"The pool's occupied," Josh called out. "Come back tomorrow." A low grumble followed his words, but soon the sound of the voices faded.

The moment was ruined. They both accepted it with reluctance and regret. Josh kissed her forehead, and she snuggled against him. The water lapped against them, and they hugged each other, their bodies entwined.

"Next time, angel," he said, tucking his finger under her chin and raising her eyes to his. "We don't stop."

Chapter Nine

About last night," Josh started, looking disgruntled and eager to talk.

"That's exactly what I want to talk to you about," Amy whispered fiercely as she joined him in the dining room the following morning. "It isn't there."

Manuela had just finished serving him a plate heaped high with hot pancakes. He waited until the housekeeper was out of the room before he spoke. "What isn't there?" Josh asked, pouring thick maple syrup over his breakfast.

"My bikini," she returned, growing frustrated. "I went down to the pool early this morning... before anyone else could find it, and my suit *wasn't there*." She was certain her cheeks were the same color as the cranberry juice he was drinking. It had been too dark to search for it the night before, and so cold when they climbed out of the water that Josh had insisted they wait until morning.

"I'm sure it'll show up," he said nonchalantly.

"But it's not there now. What could have possibly happened to it?" Naturally, he was unconcerned. It wasn't *his* swimsuit that was missing. The fact that he was having so much trouble suppressing a smile wasn't helping matters, either.

"It's probably stuck in the pump."

"Don't be ridiculous," she countered, not appreciating his miserable attempt at humor. "The pump would never suck up anything that big."

"Trust me, honey. There wasn't enough material in that bikini to cover a baby's bottom. Personally, I don't want to be the one to explain to your father how it got there when he has to call in a plumber."

"Funny. Very funny."

She'd just pulled out a chair to sit across the table from him when the phone rang. She turned, prepared to answer, when the second ring was abruptly cut off.

"Manuela must have gotten it," she said, noting that Josh had set his fork aside as if he expected the call to be for him. Sure enough, a couple of moments later, the plump Mexican cook came rushing into the dining room. "The phone is for you, Mr. Josh," she said with a heavy accent.

Josh nodded, and he cast a glance in Amy's direction. She could have sworn his eyes held an apologetic look, which was ridiculous, since there was nothing to feel contrite about. He scooted away from the table and stood with the aid of his cane. Her gaze followed him, and she was surprised when he walked into the library and deliberately closed the door.

"Well," Amy muttered aloud, pouring herself a cup of coffee. So the man had secrets. To the best of her knowledge, Josh had never received or made a phone call the entire time he had spent with them. But then, she wasn't with him twenty-four hours a day, either.

An eternity passed before Josh returned—Amy was on her second cup of coffee—but she was determined to drink the entire pot if it took that long.

He was leaning heavily upon the cane, his progress slow as he made his way into the dining room. This time his eyes avoided hers.

"Your breakfast is cold," she said, standing behind her chair. "Would you like me to ask Manuela to make you another plate?"

"No, thanks," he said, and his frown deepened.

Amy strongly suspected his scowl had little or nothing to do with his cold breakfast.

"Is anything the matter?" She would have swallowed her tongue before she'd directly inquire about the phone call, but something was apparently troubling Josh, and she wanted to help if she could.

"No," he said.

He gave her a brief smile that was meant to hearten her, but didn't. His unwillingness to share, plus his determined scowl, heightened her curiosity. Then, in a heartbeat, Amy knew.

"That was Jasmine, wasn't it?" Until that moment she'd put the other woman completely out of her mind, refusing to acknowledge the possibility of Josh loving someone else. It shocked her now that she had been so blind.

"Jasmine?"

"In the hospital you murmured her name several times . . . apparently you had the two of us confused."

"Amy, I don't know anyone named Jasmine." His eyes held hers with reassuring steadiness.

"Then why would you repeat her name when you were only half-conscious?"

"Good grief, I don't know," he returned resolutely.

He looked like he was about to say something more, but Amy hurried on. "Then I don't need to worry about you leaving me for another woman?" She gave a small laugh, not understanding his mood. It was as if he had erected a concrete wall between them, and she had to shout to gain his attention.

"I'm not going to leave you for another woman." His eyes softened as they rested on her, then pooled with regret. "But I *am* leaving you."

He stated it so casually, as if he was discussing breakfast, as if it was something of little consequence in their lives. Amy felt a fist closing around her heart, the winds of his discontent whipping up unspoken fears.

"I'm sorry, Angel Eyes."

She didn't doubt his contrition was sincere. She closed her hands deliberately over the back of the dining room chair in front of her. "I . . . I don't think I understand."

"That was SunTech on the phone."

Amy swallowed tightly, debating whether she should say anything. The decision was made simultaneously with the thought. She had to! She couldn't silently stand by and do nothing.

"You couldn't possibly mean to suggest you're going back to work? Josh, you can't—you're not physically capable of it. Good grief, this is only the first day you haven't used your crutches."

"I'll be gone as soon as I've finished packing."

She blinked, noting that he hadn't bothered to respond to her objections. He never intended to discuss his plans with her. He told her, and she was to accept them.

"Where?" she asked, feeling sick to her stomach, her head and her heart numb.

"Texas."

She sighed with relief; Texas wasn't so far. "How long?" she asked next.

"What does it matter?"

"I...I'd like to know how long it will be before you can come back."

He tensed, his back as straight as a flagpole. "I won't be coming back."

"I see." He was closing himself off from her, blocking her out of his life as if she was nothing more than a passing fancy. The pain wrapped itself around her like ivy climbing up the base of a tree, choking out its life by degrees.

Without another word of explanation, Josh turned and started to walk away from her.

"You intend to forget you ever knew me, don't you?"

He paused in the doorway, his back to her, his shoulders stiff and proud. "No."

Amy didn't understand any of this. Only a few hours before he'd held her in his arms, loved her, laughed with her. And now...now, he was casually turning and strolling out of her life with little or no excuse. It didn't make any sense.

Several minutes passed before Amy had the strength to move. When she did, she vaulted past Josh as he slowly made his way up the stairs one at a time. Poised at the top, she forced a smile to her lips, although they trembled with barely suppressed emotion.

"You can't leave yet," she said with a saucy grin, placing a hand on her hip and doing her best to look sophisticated and provocative. "We have some unfinished business. Remember?"

"No, we don't."

"Josh, you're the one who claimed that the next time we don't stop."

"There isn't going to be a next time."

He was so cold, so callous, so determined. Removing her hand from her hip, Amy planted it on her forehead, her thoughts rumbling in her mind, deep and dark. Lost. "I think I'm missing out on something here. Last night—"

Josh stopped her with a glare, telling her with his eyes what he said every time he touched her. *Last night was a mistake.*

"All right," she continued, undaunted. "Last night probably shouldn't have happened. But it did. It has in the past, and I was hoping—well, never mind, you know what I was hoping."

"Amy..."

"I want to know what's so different now? Why this morning instead of yesterday or the day before? It's as though you can't get away from me fast enough. Why? Did I do something to offend you? If so, I think we should talk about it and clear the air...instead of this."

He reached the top of the stairs, his gaze level with her own. He tried to disguise it, but Amy saw the pain in his eyes, the regret.

"The last thing I want to do is hurt you, Amy."

"Good, then don't."

He cupped her face in his hand and gazed deeply into her eyes as if to tell her that if there had been any way to avoid this, he would have chosen it. He dropped his hand and backed up two small steps. Once more, Amy noted how sluggish his movements were, but this time she guessed it wasn't his leg that was bothering him, but his heart. She looked into his eyes and saw so many things she was certain he meant to hide from her. Confusion. Guilt. Rationalization.

Without another word, he walked past her and to his room. Not knowing what else to do, she followed him.

"You can't tell me you don't love me," she said, stepping inside after him. Immediately, her eyes fell on the open suitcase sitting atop the bed and a sick, dizzying feeling assaulted her. Josh had intended to leave even before the phone call, otherwise his suitcase wouldn't be where it was. "You *do* love me," she repeated, more forcefully this time. "I know you do."

He didn't answer her, apparently unwilling to admit his feelings either way.

"It's the money, isn't it? That damnable pride of yours is causing all this, and it's ridiculous. I could care less if you have a dime to your name. I love you, and I'm not going to stop loving you for the next fifty years. If you're so eager to go to Texas, then fine, I'll go with you. I don't need a fancy house and a big car to be happy...not when I have you."

"You're not following me to Texas or anyplace else," he said harshly, his words coated with steel. "I want that understood right now." While he was speaking, he furiously stuffed clothes into the open piece of luggage, his movements abrupt and hurried.

Amy walked over to the window and gripped her hands behind her back, her long nails cutting into her palms. "If you are worried about Dad's—"

"It isn't the money," he said curtly.

"Then what is it?" she cried, losing patience.

He pressed his lips together, and a muscle leaped in his lean jaw.

"Josh," she cried. "I want to know. I have the right, at least. If you want to walk out of my life, then that's your business, but tell me why. I've got to know."

He closed his eyes and when he opened them again, they were filled with a new determination, a new strength. "It's you. We're completely different kinds of people. I told you when we met I had no roots, and that's exactly the way I like my life. I like jobs that take me around the world and offer fresh challenges. You need a man who's going to be a father to those babies you talked about once. And it's not going to be me, sweetheart."

She flinched at the harsh way he used the term of affection. Sucking in her breath, she tried again. "When two people love each other, they can learn to compromise. I don't want to chain you to Seattle. If you want to travel, then I'll go with you wherever you want."

"You?" he snickered once. "You're used to living the life-styles of the rich and famous. Jetting off in your daddy's plane, shopping in Paris, skiing in Switzerland. Forget it, Amy. Within a month, you'd be bored out of your mind."

"Josh, how can you say that? Okay, I can understand why you'd think I'm a spoiled rich kid, and…and you're right, our life-styles *are* different, but we're compatible in other ways," she rushed on, growing desperate. "You only have to think about what . . . what nearly happened in the pool to realize that."

He paused, and his short laugh revealed no amusement. "That's another thing," he said coldly. "You with your hot little body, looking for experience. I'm telling you right now, I'm not going to be the one to give it to you."

"You seemed willing enough last night," she countered, indignation overcoming the hurt his words caused.

He granted her that much with a cocky grin. "I thank God your gardener's son showed up when he did, otherwise there could be more than one unpleasant complication to our venture into that pool."

"I'm not looking for experience, Josh, I'm looking for love."

"A twenty-four year-old virgin always coats her first time with thoughts of love—it makes it easier to justify later. It isn't love we share, Amy, it's a healthy dose of good old-fashioned lust." He stuffed a shirt inside his suitcase so forcefully it was a miracle the luggage remained intact. "When it comes to making love, you're suffering from a little retarded growth. The problem is, you don't fully realize what you're asking for, and when you find out, it's going to shock you."

"You haven't shocked me."

"Trust me, I could."

He said this with a harshly indrawn breath that was sharp enough to make Amy recoil.

"Sex isn't romance, Angel Eyes, it's hot mouths and grinding hips and savage kisses. At least it is with me, and I'm not looking to initiate a novice."

"It seems we've done our share of . . . that."

"You wouldn't leave me alone, would you? I tried to stay out of your way. I went to great pains to be sure we wouldn't be alone together—to remove ourselves from the temptation. But you would have none of that—you threw yourself at me at every opportunity."

That was true enough, and Josh knew it.

"Hell, I'm a man, what was I supposed to do, ignore you? So I slipped a couple of times. I tried to ward you off, but you were so eager to lose your virginity, you refused to listen. Now the painful part comes. Good God, I was as much of a gentleman as I could be under the circumstances. It wasn't as if I didn't try." He slammed the lid of his suitcase closed, shaking the bed in the process.

A polite knock sounded at the door, and Josh turned slowly toward it. "Yes, what is it, Manuela?"

"Mr. Josh, there is taxi here for you."

"Thank you. Tell him I'll be down in a couple of minutes."

Amy blinked as fast as she could to keep the burning tears from spilling down her cheeks. "You're really leaving me, aren't you?" She was frozen with shock.

"Damn it," Josh shouted. "You knew the score when I met you. I haven't lied to you, Amy, not once. Did you think I was joking when I told you I was walking out that door and I didn't plan on coming back? Accept it. Don't make this any more difficult than it already is."

"Go then," she whispered, pride coming to her rescue. "If you can live with the thought of another man holding and kissing me and making love with me then . . . go." *Go,* she cried silently, *before I beg you to stay.*

For a moment, Josh stood stock-still. Then he reached for his suitcase, closing his fingers viciously around the handle, and dragged it across the bed. He held it in one hand and his cane in the other. Without looking at her, he headed toward the stairs.

Amy stood where she was, tears raining down her face in a storm of fierce emotion. By the time the shock had started to dissipate and she ran to the head of the stairs, Josh was at the front door.

"Josh," she cried, bracing her hands against the railing.

He paused, but he didn't turn and look at her.

"Go ahead and walk out that door . . . I'm not going to do anything to stop you."

"That's encouraging."

She closed her eyes to the stabbing pain. "I . . . I just wanted you to know that you can have all the adventures you want and travel to every corner of the world and even . . . and even make love to a thousand women."

"I intend on doing exactly that."

He was facing her now, but the tears had blinded her and all she could make out was a watery image. "Live your life and I'll . . . I'll live mine, and we'll probably never see each other again, but . . . I swear to you . . . one day you're going to regret this." Her shoulders shook with sobs. "One day you're going to look back and think of all that you threw away and realize . . ." She paused, unable to go on, and wiped the moisture from her eyes.

"Can I go now?"

"Stop being so cruel."

"It's the only thing you'll accept," he shouted, his anger vibrating all the way up the stairs. He turned from her once more.

"Josh," she cried, her hands knotting into tight fists at her sides.

"Now what?"

The air between them crackled with electricity and the longest moment of her life passed before she could speak. "Don't come back," she told him. "Don't ever come back."

Josh rubbed his eyes with his thumb and index finger and sagged in the seat of the yellow cab.

"Where to, mister?"

"Sea-Tac Airport," Josh instructed. His insides felt like a bowl of overcooked oatmeal tossed in a camp fire. Surviving the explosion had been nothing compared to saying goodbye to Amy. He would gladly have run into another burning building rather than walk away from her again. He had to leave, he had known that the minute he climbed out of the pool the night before. It was either get the hell out of her life before their lovemaking went too far or marry her.

For both their sakes, he was leaving.

But it hadn't been easy. The memory of the way her eyes had clouded with pain would haunt him until the day he died. He shut his mind to the image of her standing at the top of the stairs. Her anguish had called to him in an age-old litany that would echo in his mind far beyond the grave.

What she said about him regretting leaving her had hit him like a blow to the solar plexus. Hell, he hadn't even been away five minutes, and the remorse struck him the way fire attacks dry timber.

She was right about him loving her, too. Josh hadn't tried to lie about his feelings. He couldn't have, because she knew. Unfortunately, loving her wouldn't make things right for them. It might have worked, they may have been able to build a life together, if she wasn't who she was—Harold Johnson's daughter. Even then Josh had his doubts. There was only one absolute in all this— he wasn't ever going to stop loving her. At least not in this lifetime.

"Hey, buddy, are you all right back there?" the cab driver asked over his shoulder. He was balding and friendly.

"I'm fine."

"You don't look so fine. You look like a man who's been done wrong by his woman. What's the matter, did she kick you out?"

Josh met the driver's question with angry silence.

"Listen, friend, if I were you, I wouldn't put up with it. Women these days need to be put in their place, if you know what I mean. Keep 'em barefoot and pregnant—that's what I always say." His laugh was as coarse as his words.

Josh closed his eyes against fresh pain. Amy's words about another man making love to her had hit their mark. Bull's-eye. If he had anything to be pleased about, it was the fact that he had left her with her innocence intact. It had come so damn close in the pool. He had managed to leave her pure and sweet for some other man to initiate into lovemaking.

A blinding light flashed through his head, and the pain was so intense that he blinked several times against its unexpected onslaught.

"Hey, friend, I know a good lawyer if you need one. From the looks of it, you two got plenty of cold cash. That makes it tough. I know a lot of people who've got money, and from what I see, it sure as hell didn't buy happiness."

"I don't need a lawyer."

The taxi driver shook his head. "That's a mistake too many men make, these days. They want to keep everything friendly for the kids' sake. You got kids?"

Josh's eyes drifted closed. Children. For a time there, soon after they had returned from Kadiri, Josh had dreamed of having children with her. He dreamed a good deal about making those babies, too. He smiled wryly. If he had learned anything in the months he had spent loving Amy, it was the ability to imagine the impossible. He would wrap those fantasies around him now the way his Aunt Hazel tucked an afghan around her shoulders in the heart of winter.

"I got two boys myself," the driver continued, apparently unconcerned with the lack of response from his passenger. "They're mostly grown now, and I don't mind telling you they turned out all right. Whatever you do, buddy, don't let the wife take those kids away from you. Fight for 'em if you got to, but fight."

Josh was battling, all right, but the war he was waging was going on inside his head. It didn't take much imagination to picture Amy's stomach swollen with his child and the joy that would radiate from her eyes when she looked at him. Only there wouldn't be any children. Because there wouldn't be any Amy. At least not for him.

"Buddy, you sure you don't want the name of that lawyer? He's good. Damn good."

"I'm sure."

The cab eased to a stop outside the airport terminal, and the chatty driver looped his arm around the back of the seat and twisted around to Josh. "Buddy, I don't mean to sound like a know-it-all, but running away isn't going to solve anything."

Josh dug out his wallet and pulled out a couple of bills. "This enough?"

"Plenty." The cabbie reached for his cash box. "No, sir, the airport is the last place in the world you should be," he muttered as he drew out a five-dollar bill.

Josh already had his hand on the door. He needed to escape before he realized how much sense this taxi driver was making. "Keep the change."

"Amy." Her father tapped gently against her bedroom door. "Sweetheart, are you all right?"

She sat with her back against the headboard, her knees drawn up. The room was dark. Maybe if she ignored him, her father would go away.

"Amy?"

She sniffled and reached for another tissue. "I'm fine," she called, hoping he would accept that and leave her alone. "Really, Dad, I'm okay." She wasn't in the mood for conversation or father-daughter talks or anything else. All she wanted was to curl up in a tight ball and bandage her wounds. The pain was still too raw to share with her father, although she loved him dearly.

Contrary to her wishes, he let himself into her room and automatically reached for the light switch. Amy squinted and covered her face. "Dad, please, I just want to be by myself for a while." It was then that she noticed the illuminated dial on her clock radio. "What are you doing home this time of day, anyway?"

"Josh phoned me from the airport on his way out of town."

"Why? So he could gloat?" she asked bitterly.

Harold Johnson sat on the edge of his daughter's bed and gently patted her shoulder. "No. He wanted to thank me for my hospitality and to say you probably needed someone about now. From the look of things, he was right."

"I'm doing quite nicely without him, so you don't need to worry." And she would—in a few months or a few years, she added mentally.

"I know you are, sweetheart."

She blew her nose and rubbed the back of her hand across her eyes. "He loves me...in my heart I know he does, and still he walked away."

"I don't doubt that, either."

"Then why?"

"I wish I knew."

"I...I don't think we'll ever know," she sobbed. "I hurt so much I want to hate him and then all I can think is that the ... the least he could have done was marry me for my money."

Her father chuckled softly and gathered her in his arms. "Listen, baby, a wise man once stated that happiness broadens our hearts, but sorrow opens our souls."

"Then you can drive a truck through mine."

He held her close. "Try to accept the fact Josh chose to leave, for whatever reason. He's gone. He told me when he first came that was his intention."

"He didn't tell me," she moaned. "Dad, I love him so much. How am I ever going to let him go?"

"The pain will get better in time, I promise you."

"Maybe," she conceded, "but it doesn't seem possible right now." Knowing Josh didn't want to marry her was difficult enough, but refusing to make love with her made his rejection all the more difficult to bear.

"Come downstairs," her father coaxed. "Sitting in your room with the drapes closed isn't helping anything."

She shook her head. "Maybe later."

"How about a trip? Take off with a friend for a while and travel."

She shook her head and wiped a tear from her cheek. "No, thanks. It isn't that I don't appreciate the offer, but I wouldn't enjoy myself. At least not now."

"Okay, baby, I understand." Gently he kissed her crown and stood.

"Dad," she called to him when he started to walk out of her room. "Did Josh say ... anything else?"

"Yes." His eyes settled on her and grew sad. "He said goodbye."

The knot in her stomach twisted so tight that she sucked in her breath to the surge of unexpected pain. "Goodbye," she repeated, and closed her eyes.

* * *

The next morning, Amy's alarm clock rang at six, rousing her from bed. She showered and dressed in her best suit, primly tucking in her hair at her nape in a loose chignon.

Her father was at the breakfast table when she joined him. His eyes rounded with surprise when she walked into the room.

"Good morning, Dad," she said, reaching for the coffee. She didn't have Josh, but she had her father. Harold Johnson had the courage of a giant and the sensitive heart of a child. Just being with him would help her find the way out of this bitter unhappiness.

"Amy." It looked as if he wasn't quite sure what to say. "It's early for you, isn't it?"

"Not anymore. Now, before we head for the office, is there anything you want to fill me in on?"

For the first time Amy could remember, her father was completely speechless.

Chapter Ten

There was a call for you earlier," Rusty Everett told Josh when he returned from lunch.

Josh's heart thudded heavily. "Did you catch the name?"

"Yeah, I wrote it down here someplace." Rusty, fifty and as Texan as they come, rummaged around his cluttered desk for several moments. "Hell, I don't know what I did with it. Whoever it was said they'd call back later."

"It didn't happen to be a woman, did it?" One that had the voice of an angel, Josh added silently. He'd gone out of his way to be damn sure Amy never wanted to see or talk to him again, and yet his heart couldn't stop longing for her.

"No, this was definitely a man."

"If you find the name, let me know."

"Right."

Leaning upon his cane, Josh made his way into the small office. Since he was still recovering from the explosion, Josh was pushing a pencil for SunTech. He didn't like being cooped up inside an office, but he didn't know if he should attribute this unyielding restlessness to the circumstances surrounding his employment or the gaping hole left in his life without Amy. He had the feeling he could be tanning on the lush white sands of a tropical paradise and still find plenty of cause for complaint.

As painful as it was to admit, there was only one place he wanted to be, and that was in Seattle with a certain angel. Instead, he was doing everything within his power to arrange a transfer to the farthest reaches of planet earth so he could escape her. The problem was, it probably wouldn't matter where he ran, his memories would always catch up with him.

He was wrong to have abruptly left her the way he did, to deliberately hurt her, but, unfortunately, he knew it was the right thing for them both, even if she didn't.

He'd been noble, but he'd behaved like a bastard.

He had to forget her, but his heart and his mind and his soul wouldn't let him.

Wiping a hand across his face, Josh leaned back in his chair and rubbed the ache from his right thigh. The pain in his leg was minute compared to the throbbing anguish that surrounded his heart.

With determination, Josh reached for the geological report he wanted to read, but his mind wasn't on oil exploration. It was on an angel who had turned his life upside down.

"Hey, Josh," Rusty called from the other room. "You've got a visitor."

Josh stood and nearly fell back into his chair in shock when Harold Johnson casually strolled into his office.

"Hello, Josh."

Amy's father greeted him as if they were sitting down to a pleasant meal together. "Mr. Johnson," Josh replied stiffly, ill at ease.

The two shook hands, eyeing each other. One confident, the other dubious, Josh noted. Without waiting for an invitation, Harold claimed the chair on the other side of the desk and crossed his legs as though he planned to sit and chat for a while. All he needed to complete the picture was a snifter of brandy and a Cuban cigar.

"What can I do for you?" Josh asked, doing his level best to keep his voice crisp and professional.

"Well, son," Harold said, and reached inside his suit jacket for the missing cigar. "I've come to talk to you about my daughter."

Vicious fingers clawed at Josh's stomach. "Don't. I made it clear to her, and to you, that whatever was between us is over."

"Just like that?"

"Just like that," Josh returned flatly, lying through clenched teeth.

A flame flickered at the end of the cigar, and Harold took several deep puffs, his full attention centered on the Havana Special. "She's doing an admirable job of suggesting the same thing."

Perhaps something was wrong. Maybe she had been hurt or was ill. Josh struggled to hide his growing concern. Amy's father wouldn't show up without a damn good reason.

"Is she all right?" Josh asked, unable to bear not knowing any longer.

Harold chuckled. "You'd be amazed at how well she's doing at pretending she never set eyes on you. She hasn't so much as mentioned your name since the day you left. She's cheerful, happy, enthusiastic. If I didn't know her so well, I could almost be fooled."

Relief brought down his guard. "She'll recover."

"Yes, I suspect so. She's keeping busy. The fact is, the girl surprised the dickens out of me the morning after you left. Bright and early she marched down the stairs, dressed in her best business suit, and claimed it was time she started earning her keep. Accounting never knew what hit them." The older man chuckled, sounding both delighted and proud.

If Amy's father had meant to shock him, he was doing an admirable job of it.

"The girl's got grit," Harold continued.

"Then why are you here?" Josh demanded.

"I came to see how you were doing, son."

"A phone call would have served as well."

"Tried that, but your friend there said you were out to lunch, and since I was in town, I thought I'd stop by so we could chat a bit before I flew home."

"How'd you know where to find me?"

Harold inhaled deeply on the cigar. "Were you in hiding?"

"Not exactly." But Josh hadn't let it be known where in Texas he was headed.

"I must say you're looking well."

"Thanks," Josh said, hiding his resentfulness. Most days he felt as though he wanted to hide under a rock. At least it would be dark and cold, and perhaps he could sleep without dreaming of Amy. The last thing he needed was a confrontation with her father, or to own up to the fact he was dying for news of her.

"Fact is, you look about as well as my daughter does."

Josh heaved a sigh and lowered his eyes to his paper-work, hoping Harold Johnson would take the hint.

"By the way," the older man said, a smile teasing the corners of his mouth, "you wouldn't happen to know anything about a swimsuit I found at the bottom of my pool the day you left, would you?"

It took a good deal to unsettle Josh, but in the course of five minutes Harold Johnson had done it twice. "I...Amy and I went swimming."

"Looks like one of you decided to skinny-dip," Harold added with an abrupt laugh.

His amusement bewildered Josh even more. "We... ah...I know it looks bad."

"That skimpy white thing must have belonged to my daughter, although I must admit that I'd no idea she had such a garment."

"Sir, I want you to know I...I didn't..."

"You don't have to explain yourself, son. My daughter's a grown woman, and if nothing happened, it's not from any lack of trying on her part, I'll wager."

Josh hadn't blushed since he was a boy, but he found himself doing so now.

"She must have been a damn tempting morsel for you to walk away from like that."

Josh swallowed with difficulty and nodded. "She was."

Harold Johnson puffed long and hard on his cigar once more, then held it away from his face and examined the end of it as if he suspected it wasn't lit. When he spoke again, his voice was nonchalant. "I knew a Powell once."

Josh stiffened. "It's a common enough name."

"This Powell was a successful stockbroker with his own firm situated on Wall Street. Ever hear of a fellow by the name of Chance Powell?"

A cold chill settled over Josh. "I've heard of him," he admitted cautiously.

"I thought you might have." Harold nodded, as if confirming the information he already knew. "He's one of the most successful brokers in the country. From what I understand he has offices in all fifty states now. There's been a real turnaround in his business in recent years. I understand he almost lost everything not too long ago, but he survived, and so did the business."

Josh didn't add anything to that. From the time he'd walked away from his father, he'd gone out of his way *not* to keep track of what was happening in his life, professional or otherwise.

"From what I know of him, he has only one child, a son."

If Harold was looking for someone to fill in the blanks, he was going to be disappointed. Josh sat with his back rigid, his mouth set in a thin line of impatience.

Harold chewed on the end of the cigar the way a child savors a candy sucker. "There was a write-up in the *Journal* several years back about Chance's son. I don't suppose you've heard of *him*?"

"I might have." Boldly Josh met the older man's stare, unwilling to give an inch.

"The article said the boy showed promise enough to be one of the brightest business minds this country has ever known. He graduated at the top of his class at MIT, took the business world by storm and revealed extraordinary insight. Then, without anyone ever learning exactly why, he packed up his bags and walked away from it all."

"He must have had his reasons."

Harold Johnson nodded. "I'm sure he did. Damn good ones to walk away from a brilliant future."

"Perhaps he was never interested in money," Josh suggested.

"That's apparently so, because I learned that he served for several years as a volunteer for the Peace Corps." Harold Johnson held the cigar between his fingers and lowered his gaze as if deep in thought. "It's unfortunate that such a keen business mind is being wasted. Fact is, I wouldn't mind having him become part of my own firm. Don't know if he'd consider it, though. What do you think?"

"I'm sure he wouldn't," Josh returned calmly.

"That's too bad." Harold Johnson heaved a small sigh. "His life could be a good deal different if he wished. Instead—" he paused and scowled at Josh "—he's wasted his talents."

"Wasted? Do you believe helping the less fortunate was squandering my—his life?"

"Not at all. I'm sure he contributed a good deal during the years he served with the Peace Corps. But the boy apparently has an abundance of talent in other areas. It's a shame he isn't serving where he's best suited." He stared directly at Josh for a lengthy, uncomfortable moment. "It would seem to me that this young man has made a habit of walking away from challenges and opportunities."

"I think you may be judging him unfairly."

"Perhaps," Amy's father conceded.

Josh remained silent. He knew what the older man was saying, but he wanted none of it.

Harold continued to chew on his cigar, apparently appreciating the taste of the fine Cuban tobacco more than he enjoyed smoking it. "I met Chance Powell several years back, and frankly, I liked the man,'' Harold continued, seeming to approach this conversation from fresh grounds.

"Frankly," Josh echoed forcefully, "I don't."

The older man's eyes took on an obstinate look. "I'm sorry to hear that."

Josh made a show of looking at his watch, hoping his guest would take the hint and leave before the conversation escalated into an argument. Harold didn't, but that wasn't any real surprise for Josh.

"Do you often meddle in another man's life, or is this a recent hobby?" Josh asked, swallowing what he could of the biting sarcasm.

The sound of the older man's laughter filled the small office. "I have to admit, it's a recent preoccupation of mine."

"Why now?"

Harold leaned forward and extinguished his cigar, rubbing it with unnecessary force in the glass ashtray that rested on the corner of Josh's crowded desk. "What's between Chance Powell and his son is their business."

"I couldn't agree with you more. Then why are you bringing it up?"

Any humor that lingered in the older man's gaze vanished like chocolates in a room filled with children. "Because both you and Amy are about to make the biggest mistakes of your lives, and I'm finding it damn difficult to sit back and watch."

"What goes on between the two of us is our concern, as well."

"I'll grant you that much." Releasing his breath, Harold stood, his look apologetic. "You're right, of course, I had no right coming here. If Amy knew, she'd probably never forgive me."

Josh's tight features relaxed. "You needn't worry that I'll tell her."

"Good."

"She's a strong woman," Josh said, standing and shaking hands with a man he admired greatly. "From everything you said, she's already started to rebound. She'll be dating again soon."

The smile on his lips lent credence to his words, but the thought of Amy with another man did things to his heart Josh didn't even want to consider. It was far better that he never know.

"Before you realize it, Amy will have found herself a decent husband who will make her a good deal happier than I ever could," Josh said, managing to sound as though he meant it.

Harold Johnson rubbed the side of his jaw in measured strokes. "That's the problem. I fear she already has."

Amy sat in the office of the accounting supervisor for Johnson Industries. Lloyd Dickins would be joining her directly, and she took a few moments to glance around his neat and orderly office. Lloyd's furniture was in keeping with the man, she noted. His room was dominated by thick, bulky pieces that were so unlike her own ultramodern furnishings. A picture of Lloyd's wife with their family was displayed on the credenza, and judging by its frame, the picture was several years old. The one photograph was all there was to fill in the blanks of Dickins's life outside the company. Perhaps his need for privacy, his effort to keep the two worlds separate, was the reason Amy had taken such a liking to Lloyd. It was apparent her father shared her opinion.

Lloyd had welcomed Amy into the accounting department, although she was convinced he had his reservations. Frankly, she couldn't blame him. She was the boss's daughter and if she was going to eventually assume her father's position, albeit years in the future, she would need to know every aspect of managing the conglomerate.

"Sorry to keep you waiting," Lloyd mumbled as he sailed into the office.

Amy swore the man never walked. But he didn't exactly run, either. His movements were abrupt, hurried, and Amy supposed it was that which gave the impression he was continually rushing from one place to the other. He was tall and thin, his face dominated by a smile that was quick and unwavering.

"I've only been waiting a minute," she answered, dismissing his apology.

"Did you have the chance to read over the Emerson report?" he asked as he claimed the seat at his desk. He reached for the file, thumbing through the pages of the summary. The margins were filled with notes and comments.

"I read it last night and then again this morning."

Lloyd Dickins nodded, looking pleased. "You've been putting in a good deal of time on this project. Quite honestly, Amy, I wasn't sure what to expect when your father told me you'd be joining my team. But after the last three weeks, I don't mind telling you, you've earned my respect."

"Thank you." She'd worked hard for this moment, and when the praise came, it felt good.

"Now," Lloyd said, leaning back in his chair, "tell me what you think?"

Amy spent the next ten minutes doing exactly that. When she'd finished, Lloyd added his own comments and insights and then called for a meeting of their department for that afternoon.

When Amy returned to her office, there were several telephone messages waiting for her. She left Chad's note for last. Chad Morton worked in marketing and had been wonderful for her. He was charming and suave and endearing, and best of all, nothing like Josh. In fact, no two men could have been more dissimilar, which suited her just fine. If she was going to forget Josh, she would have to do it with someone who was his complete opposite.

Chad was the type of man who would be content to smoke his pipe in front of a fireplace for the remainder of his life. He was mashed potatoes and roast beef, a hot tub and BMW personality.

"Chad, it's Amy." She spoke into the receiver. "I got your message."

"Hi, Angel Face."

Amy closed her eyes to the sudden and unexpected flash of pain. She was forced to bite her tongue to keep from asking him not to call her anything that had to do with angels. That had been Josh's line, and she was doing everything within her power to push every thought of him from her life.

"Are you free for dinner tonight?" Chad continued. "Betty and Bob phoned and want to know if we can meet them at the country club at six. We can go dancing afterward."

"Sure," Amy responded quickly, "why not? It sounds like fun." Keeping busy, she'd discovered, was the key. If she wasn't learning everything she could about her father's business, she was throwing herself into social events with the energy of a debutante with a closet full of prom dresses.

Rarely did she spend time at home anymore. Every room was indelibly stamped with memories of Josh and the long weeks he had spent recovering there. She would have given anything to completely wipe out the time spent at his side, but simultaneously she held the memories tightly to her breast, treasuring each minute he'd been in her life.

She was mixed up, confused, hurting and pretending otherwise.

It seemed Josh had left his mark in each and every room of her home. She couldn't walk into the library and not feel an emptiness that stabbed deep into her soul.

Only when she ventured near the pool did she feel his presence stronger than his absence, and she left almost immediately, rather than have to deal with her rumbling emotions.

When Amy arrived home that evening, she was surprised to discover her father sitting in the library in front of the fireplace, his feet up and a blanket draped over his lap. It was so unusual to find him resting that the sight stopped her abruptly in the hallway.

"Dad," she said, stepping into the room. "When did you get back?" Still perplexed, but pleased to see him, she leaned over to affectionately kiss his cheek. He'd been away several days on a business trip and wasn't expected home until the following afternoon.

"I landed an hour ago," Harold answered, smiling softly at her.

Amy removed her coat and curled up in a chair beside him. "I didn't think you'd be home until tomorrow night. Chad phoned, and we're going out to dinner and dancing. You don't mind, do you?''

He didn't answer her for several elongated moments, as if he was searching for the right words. This, too, was unlike him, and Amy wondered at his mood.

"You're seeing a good deal of Chad Morton, aren't you? The two of you are gallivanting around town every night of the week, it seems. It wouldn't surprise me if he brought up the subject of marriage soon."

Amy sidestepped the question. As a matter of fact, she'd been thinking those same thoughts herself. She *had* been seeing a good deal of Chad. He'd asked her out the first day she started working at Johnson Industries, and they'd been together nearly every night since.

"Do you object?" she asked pointedly. "Chad would make an excellent husband. He comes from a good family, and seems nice enough."

"True, but you don't love him."

"Who said anything about love?" Amy asked, forcing a light laugh. As far as she was concerned, falling in love had been greatly overrated.

If she was going to become involved with a man she would much rather it was with someone like Chad. He was about as exciting as one-coat paint, but irrefutably stable. If there was anything she needed in her life, it was someone she could depend on who would love her for the next fifty years without demands, without questions.

As an extra bonus, there would never be any threat of her falling head over heels for Chad Morton and making a fool of herself the way she had for Josh Powell. No, it wasn't love, but it was comfortable.

Her father reached for his brandy, and Amy poured herself a glass of white wine, savoring these few minutes alone with him. They seldom sat and talked anymore, but the fault was mainly her own. In fact, she had avoided moments such as this. Her biggest fear was that he would say something about Josh, and she wouldn't be able to deal with it.

"I may not love Chad, but he's nice," she answered simply, hoping that would appease the question burning in her father's deep blue eyes.

"Nice," Harold repeated, his smile sad and off-center. He made the word sound trivial and weak, as if he was describing the man himself.

"Chad works for you," she said as a means of admonishment.

"True enough."

"So how was the trip?" she asked, turning the course of the conversation. She hadn't said she would accept Chad's proposal when he offered it, only that she fully expected him to tender one soon. She hadn't made up her mind one way or the other on how she would answer such a question. A good deal would depend on what her father thought. Since the two men would be working closely together in the future, it would be best if they liked and respected each other . . . the way Josh and her father seemed to have felt.

Josh again. She closed her eyes to the thought of him, forgetting for the moment that he was out of her life and wouldn't be back.

Once more her father hesitated before answering her question. "The trip was interesting."

"Oh?" Rarely did her father hedge, but he seemed to be doing his fair share of it this evening.

His gaze pulled hers the same way a magnet attracts steel. "From Atlanta I flew down to Texas."

Amy rotated the crystal stem between her open palms, her heart perking like a brewing pot of coffee. Josh had claimed he was heading for Texas, but it was a big state and . . .

She blinked a couple of times, hoping desperately that she had misread her father, but one look from him confirmed her worst suspicion. Instantly, her throat went dry and her tongue felt as if it was glued to the roof of her mouth.

"You . . . talked to Josh, didn't you?"

Without the least bit of hesitation, Harold Johnson nodded, but his eyes were weary, as if he anticipated a confrontation.

Her lashes fluttered closed at the intense feelings of hurt and betrayal. "How could you?" she cried, bolting to her feet. Unable to stand still, she set the wineglass aside and started pacing the room, her movements crisp enough to impress the military.

"He put on a brave front—the same way you've been doing for the last three weeks."

Amy wasn't listening. "In all my life, I've never questioned or doubted anything you've ever done. I love you . . . I trusted you." Her voice was trembling so badly that it was amazing he could even understand her. "How could you?"

"Amy, sit down, please."

"No!" she shouted. The sense of betrayal was so strong, she didn't think she could remain in the same room with him any longer. Through the years, Amy had always considered her father to be her most loyal friend. He was the safe port she steered toward in times of trouble. Since she was a child he'd been the one who pointed out the rainbow at the end of a cloudburst. He was the compass who directed the paths of her life.

Until this moment, she had never doubted anything he'd done for her.

"What possible reason could you have to contact Josh?" she demanded. "Were you looking to humiliate me more? Is that it? It's a wonder he didn't laugh in your face ... Perhaps he did, in which case it would serve you right."

"Amy, sweetheart, that isn't the reason I saw Josh. You should know that."

Furious, she brushed away the tears that sprang so readily to her eyes and seared a wet trail down her cheeks. "I suppose you told him I was wasting away for want of him? No doubt you boosted his arrogance by claiming I'm still crazy about him ... and that I'll probably never stop loving him."

"Amy, please—"

"Wasn't his leaving humiliation enough?" she shouted. "Who ... gave you the right to rub salt in my wounds? Didn't you think I was hurting enough?" Without waiting for his reply, Amy stormed out of the library, so filled with righteous anger that she didn't stop until she was in her bedroom.

No more than a minute had passed before her father pounded on her door.

"Amy, please, let me talk to you."

"No ... just go away."

"But I need to explain. You're right, I probably shouldn't have gone to see Josh without talking with you about it first, but there was something I needed to discuss with him."

Although she remained furious, she opened her bedroom door and folded her arms across her chest. "What possible reason could you have to talk to Joshua Powell ... if it didn't directly involve me?"

Her father stood just outside her door, a sheen of perspiration moistening his pale forehead and upper lip. He probably shouldn't have come racing up the stairs after her. He looked ashen, and his breathing was labored, but Amy chose to ignore that, too angry to care.

"Dad?" she repeated, bracing her hands against her hips. "Why did you talk to Josh?"

Her father's responding smile was weak at best. "I have a feeling you aren't going to like this, either." He hesitated and wiped a hand across his brow. "I went to offer him a job."

"You did what?" It demanded everything within Amy not to explode on the spot. She stood frozen for a moment, then buried her face in her hands.

"It isn't as bad as it seems, sweetheart. Joshua Powell is fully qualified. I was just looking to—"

"I know what you were trying to do," Amy cried. "You were looking to *buy* him for me!" Before it had been her voice that trembled. Now her entire body shook with outrage and fury. Her knees didn't feel as if they were going to support her any longer.

But that didn't stop her from charging across the room to her closet and throwing open the doors with every ounce of strength she possessed. She dragged out her suitcases and slammed them across the bed.

"Amy, what are you doing?"

"Leaving. This house. Johnson Industries. And you."

Her calm, rational father looked completely undone. If he was colorless before, he went deathly pale now. "Sweetheart, there's no reason for you to move out." The look in his eyes was desperate. "There's no need to over-react . . . Josh turned down the offer."

The added humiliation was more than Amy could handle.

"Of course he did. He didn't want me before. What made you think he would now?" Without stopping, she emptied her drawers, tossing her clothes in the open suitcase, unable to escape fast enough.

"Amy, please, don't do anything rash."

"Rash?" she repeated, hiccuping on a sob. "I should have moved out years ago, but I was under the impression that we . . . shared something special . . . like trust, mutual respect . . . love. Until tonight, I believed you—"

"Amy."

Something in the strangled way he uttered her name alerted her to the fact something was wrong. Something was very, very wrong. She whirled around in time to see her father grip his chest, roll back his eyes and slump unconscious to the floor.

Chapter Eleven

Josh lowered the week-old *Wall Street Journal* and let the newspaper rest on his lap while his mind whirled with troubled concern. Mingling with his worries was an abundance of ideas, most of them maverick—but then he had been considered one in his time.

"What part of the world are you headed for now, dear?" his Aunt Hazel inquired, her soft voice curious. She sat across the living room from him, her fingers pushing the knitting needles the way a secretary worked a keyboard. Her white hair was demurely pinned at the back of her head, and tiny wisps framed her oval face. Her features, although marked with age, were soft and gentle. Her outer beauty had faded years before, but the inner loveliness shone brighter each time he stopped to visit. Without much difficulty, Josh could picture Amy resembling his aunt in fifty or so years.

"I'm hoping to go back to Kadiri," he answered her, elbowing thoughts of Amy from his mind.

"Isn't that the place that's been in the news recently?" she asked, sounding worried. "There's so much unrest in this world. I have such a difficult time understanding why people can't get along with one another." She pointedly glanced in his direction, her hands resting in her lap as her tender brown eyes challenged him.

Over the years, Josh had become accustomed to his aunt inserting barbed remarks, thinly veiled, about his relationship with his father. Josh generally ignored them, pretending he didn't understand what she meant. He preferred to avoid a confrontation. As far as he was concerned, his Aunt Hazel was his only relative, and he loved her dearly.

"What's that you're reading so intently?"

Josh's gaze fell to the newspaper. *"The Wall Street Journal."* Knowing his aunt would put the wrong connotation into the subject matter, since he normally avoided anything that had to do with the financial world, he hurried to explain. "I have a . . . friend, Harold Johnson, who owns and operates a large conglomerate. With all the traveling I do, it's difficult to keep in contact with him, so I keep tabs on him by occasionally checking to see how his stock is doing."

"And what does that tell you?"

"Several things."

"Like what, dear?" she asked conversationally.

Josh wasn't certain his aunt would understand all the ins and outs of the corporate world, so he explained it as best he could in simple terms. "Stock prices tell me how he's doing financially."

"I see. But you've been frowning for the last fifteen minutes. Is something wrong with your friend?"

Josh picked up the newspaper and made a ceremony of folding it precisely in fourths. "His bond rating has just been lowered."

"That's not good?"

"No. There's an article here that states that Johnson Industries' stock price is currently depressed, which means the value has fallen below its assets. With several long-term bonds maturing, the cost of rolling them over may become prohibitive."

His Aunt Hazel returned to her knitting. "Yes, but what does all that mean?"

Josh struggled to put it into terminology his aunt would understand. "Trouble, mostly. Basically it means that Johnson Industries is a prime candidate for a hostile takeover. He may be forced into selling the controlling interest of the business he's struggled to build over a lifetime to someone else."

"That doesn't seem fair. If a man works hard all his years to build up a business, it's not right that someone else can waltz right in and take over."

"Little in life is fair anymore," Josh said, unable to disguise his bitterness.

"Oh, Josh, honestly." His aunt rested her hands in her lap and slowly shook her head, pressing her lips together tightly. "You have become such a pessimist over the years. If I wasn't so glad to see you when you came to visit me, I'd take delight in shaking some sense into you."

Although his aunt was serious, Josh couldn't help laughing outright. "Harold's going to be just fine. He's a strong man with a lot of connections. The sharks are circling, but they'll soon start looking for weaker prey."

"Good. I hate the thought of your friend losing his business."

"So do I." Setting the newspaper aside, Josh closed his eyes, battling down the surge of long-forgotten excitement. The adrenaline had started to pound through his blood the minute he had picked up the *Wall Street Journal*. It had been years since he had allowed himself the luxury of remembering the life he'd left behind. Since the final showdown with his father, he had done everything he could to forget how much he loved plowing into problems with both hands, such as the one Johnson Industries was currently experiencing. Before he realized what he was doing, his mind was churning out ways to deal with this difficulty.

Releasing his breath, Josh closed his mind to the thought of offering any advice to Amy's father. The cord had been cut, and he couldn't turn back now.

"Your father is looking well," his aunt took obvious delight in informing him.

Josh ignored her. He didn't want to discuss Chance, and Aunt Hazel knew it, but she did her best to introduce the subject of his father as naturally as possible.

"He asked about you."

Josh scoffed before he thought better of it.

"He loves you, Josh," Hazel insisted sharply. "If the pair of you weren't so damn proud, you could settle this unpleasantness in five minutes. But I swear, you're no better than he is."

The fierce anger that shot through Josh was hot enough to boil his blood and, unable to stop his tongue, he blurted out, "I may not be a multimillionaire, but at least I'm not a crook. My father should be in prison right now, and you damn well know it. You both seem to think I was supposed to ignore the fact that Chance Powell is a liar and a cheat."

"Josh, please, I didn't mean to reopen painful wounds. It's just that I've seen you fly from one end of the world to the other in an effort to escape this difficulty with your father. I hardly know you anymore... I can't understand how you can turn away from everything that ever had any value to you."

The older woman looked pale, and Josh immediately regretted his outburst. "I'm sorry, Aunt Hazel, I shouldn't have raised my voice to you. Now, what was it you said you were cooking for dinner?"

"Crow," she told him, her eyes twinkling.

"I beg your pardon?"

She laughed softly and shook her head. "I seem to put my foot in my mouth every time I try to talk some sense into you. No matter what you do with the rest of your life, Joshua, I want you to know I'll always love you. You're the closest thing to a son I've ever had. Forgive an old woman for sticking her nose where it doesn't belong."

Josh set aside the paper and walked over to sit on the arm of her overstuffed chair. Then he leaned over and kissed her cheek. "If you can forgive me for my sharp tongue, we'll call it square."

That night, Josh wasn't able to sleep. He lay on the mattress with his hands supporting the back of his head and stared into empty space. Every time he closed his eyes, he saw Harold Johnson sitting across the desk from him, discussing his current financial difficulties. Amy's father was probably in the most delicate position of his business career. The sheer force of the older man's personality was enough to ward off all but the most bloodthirsty sharks. But Josh didn't know how long Harold could keep them at bay. For Amy's sake, he hoped nothing else would go wrong.

His first inclination had been to contact her father with a few suggestions. But Harold Johnson didn't need him, and for that matter, neither did Amy. According to her father, she was seriously dating someone else. In fact, he had claimed she would probably be wearing a wedding ring before long.

Josh hadn't asked any questions, although he would have given his right hand to have learned the name of the man who had swept her off her feet so soon after he had left. More than likely, Josh wouldn't have known the other man, and it wouldn't have mattered if he had.

When he had flown out of Seattle, Josh had hoped Amy would hurry and fall in love with someone else, so there was no reason for him to be unsettled now. This was exactly what he had wanted to happen. So why was he being eaten alive with regrets and doubts?

The answer was obvious. He was never going to stop loving Amy. For the first time since his conversation with her father, he was willing to admit what a fool he had been to have honestly believed he had meant it. Just the thought of her even *kissing* another man filled him with such anger that he clenched his fists with impotent rage.

If that wasn't bad enough, envisioning Amy making love with her newfound friend was akin to having his skin ripped off his body one strip at a time. The irony of this was that Amy had told him as much. She'd stood at the top of her stairs and shouted it to him, he recalled darkly. *If you can live with the thought of another man holding and kissing me and making love to me then . . . go.*

Josh *had* walked away from her, but she had been right. The thought caused him more agony than his injuries from the explosion ever had.

Harold Johnson's words came back to haunt him, as well. They had been talking, and Amy's father had stared directly at him and claimed: *This young man has made a habit of walking away from challenges and opportunities.*

At the time it had been all Josh could do not to defend himself. He had let the comment slide rather than force an argument. Now the truth of the older man's words hit him hard, leaving him defenseless.

Josh couldn't deny that he had walked away from his father, turned his back on the life he had once enjoyed, and had been running ever since. Even his love for Amy hadn't been strong enough to force him to deal with that pain. Instead, he had left her and then been forced to deal with another more intense agony. His life felt like an empty shell, as if he were going through the motions, but rejecting all the benefits.

In his own cavalier way, he'd carelessly thrown away the very best thing that had ever happened to him.

Love. Amy's love.

Closing his eyes to the swell of bitter regret, Josh lay in bed trying to decide what he was going to do about it. If anything.

He didn't know if he could casually walk into Amy's life after the way he had so brutally abandoned her. The answer was as difficult to face as the question had been.

Perhaps it would be best to leave her to what happiness she had found for herself.

Doubts pounded at him from every corner until he realized sleep would be impossible. Throwing back the blankets, he climbed out of bed, dressed and wandered into the living room. His aunt's bedroom door had been left slightly ajar, and he could hear her snoring softly in the background. Instead of being irritated, he was comforted by the knowledge that she was his family. He didn't visit her as often as he should, and he was determined to do so from now on.

Josh sat in the dark for several minutes, reviewing his options with Amy and her father. He needed time to carefully think matters through.

In the wee hours of the morning, he turned on the television, hoping to find a movie that would help him fall asleep. Instead, he fiddled with the cable selector until he found a station that broadcast twenty-four-hour financial news. The article in the *Wall Street Journal* was a week old. A great many things could have happened to Johnson Industries in seven days. It wasn't likely that he would learn anything, but he was curious nonetheless.

"Josh, what are you doing up at this time of night?" his aunt demanded, sounding very much like a mother scolding her twelve-year-old son. She stood and held the back of her hand over her mouth as she yawned. She was dressed in a lavender terry-cloth robe that was tightly cinched at the waist, and her soft hair was secured with a thin black net.

"I couldn't sleep."

"How about some warm milk? It always works for me."

"Only if you add some chocolate and join me."

His aunt chuckled and headed toward the kitchen. "Do you want a bedtime story while I'm at it?"

Josh grinned. "It wouldn't hurt."

She stuck her head around the corner. "That's what I thought you'd say."

Josh stood, prepared to follow her. He walked toward the television, intent on turning it off, when he heard the news. For one wild moment, he stood frozen in shock and disbelief.

"Aunt Hazel," he called once he found his voice. "You'd better cancel the hot chocolate."

"Whatever for?" she asked, but stopped abruptly when she turned and saw him. "Josh, what's happened? My dear boy, you're as pale as a ghost."

"It's my friend. The one I was telling you about earlier—he's had a heart attack and isn't expected to live."

For most of the evening, Josh had been debating what he should do. He had struggled with indecision and uncertainty, trying to decide if it would be best to leave well enough alone and let both Amy and her father go on with their lives. At the same time, he had begun to wonder if he could face life without his Angel Eyes at his side.

Now the matter had been taken out of his hands. There was only one option left to him, and that was to return. If Johnson Industries had been a prime candidate for a hostile takeover *before* Harold's heart attack, it was even more vulnerable now. Sharks always went after the weakest prey, and Johnson Industries lay before them with its throat exposed. Josh's skills might be rusty, but they were intact, and he knew he could help.

Amy would need him now, too. Father and daughter had always been especially close, and losing Harold now would devastate her.

"Josh." His aunt interrupted his musings, her hand on his forearm. "What are you going to do?"

Josh's eyes brightened and he leaned forward to place a noisy kiss on his aunt's cheek. "What I should have done weeks ago—get married."

"Married? But to whom?" A pair of dark brown eyes rounded with surprise. Flustered, she patted her hair. "Actually, I don't care who it is as long as I get an invitation to the wedding."

* * *

Like a limp rag doll, Amy sat and stared at the wall outside her father's hospital room. He was in intensive care, and she was only allowed to see him for a few minutes every hour. She lived for those brief moments when she could hold his hand and gently reassure him of her love, hoping to lend him some strength. For three days he'd lain in a coma, unable to respond.

Not once in those long, tedious days had she left the hospital. Not to sleep, not to eat, not to change clothes. She feared the minute she left him, he would slip into death and she wouldn't be there to prevent it.

Hurried footsteps sounded on the polished floor of the hospital corridor, but she didn't turn to see who was coming. So many had sat by her side, staff requesting information, asking questions she didn't want to answer, friends and business associates. But Amy had sent them all away. Now she felt so alone and so terribly weary.

The footsteps slowed.

"Amy."

Her heart thudded to a stop. "Josh?" Before she was entirely certain how it happened, she was securely tucked in his embrace, her arms wrapped around his neck and her face buried in his chest, breathing in his strength the way desert-dry soil drinks in the rain.

For the first time since her father's heart attack, she gave in to the luxury of tears. They poured from her eyes like water rushing over a dam. Her shoulders jerked with sobs, and she held on to Josh with every ounce of strength she possessed.

Josh's hands were in her hair, and his lips moved over her temple, whispering words she couldn't hear over the sound of her own weeping. It didn't matter; he was there, and she needed him. God had known and had sent him to her side.

"It's my fault," she wailed with a grief that came from the bottom of her soul, trying to explain what had happened. "Everything is my fault."

"No, angel, it isn't, I'm sure it couldn't be."

No one seemed to understand that. No one, and she was too weak to explain. Stepping back, she wiped the tears from her eyes, although it did little good because more poured down her face. "I caused this...I did...we were arguing and...and I was so angry, so hurt that I wanted to...move out and...that was when it happened."

Josh gripped her shoulders, and applying a light pressure, he lowered her into the chair. He squatted in front of her and took both her hands between his, rubbing them. It was then that Amy realized how cold she felt. Shivering and sniffling, she leaned forward enough to rest her forehead against the solid strength of his shoulder.

His arms were around her immediately.

"He's going to be all right," Josh assured her softly.

"No...he's going to die. I know he is, and I'll never be able to tell him how sorry I am."

"Amy," Josh said, gripping the sides of her head and raising her face. "Your father loves you so much, don't you think he already knows you're sorry?"

"I...I'm not sure anymore."

She swayed slightly and would have fallen if Josh hadn't caught her.

He murmured something she couldn't understand and firmly gripped her waist. "When was the last time you had anything to eat?"

She blinked, not remembering.

"Angel," he said gently, "you've got to take care of yourself, now more than ever. Your father needs to wake up and discover you standing over him with a bright smile on your face and your eyes full of love."

She nodded. That was exactly how she pictured the scene in her own mind, when she allowed herself to believe that he would come out of this alive.

"I'm taking you home."

"No." A protest rose automatically to her lips, and she shook her head with fierce determination.

"I'm going to have Manuela cook you something to eat and then I'm going to tuck you in bed and let you sleep. When you wake up, we'll talk. We have a good deal to discuss, Angel Eyes."

Something in the back of her head told Amy that she shouldn't be listening to Josh, that she shouldn't trust him. But she was so very tired, and much too exhausted to listen to the cool voice of reason.

She must have fallen asleep in the car on the way home from the hospital because the next thing she knew, they were parked outside her home and Josh was coming around to the passenger side to help her out.

He didn't allow her to walk, but gently lifted her into his arms as if she weighed less than a child and carried her in the front door.

"Manuela," he shouted.

The plump housekeeper came rushing into the entryway at the sound of Josh's voice. She took one look at him and mumbled something low and fervent in Spanish.

"Could you make something light for Amy and bring it to her room? She's on the verge of collapse."

"Right away," Manuela said, wiping her hands dry on her blue apron.

"I'm not hungry," Amy felt obliged to inform them. She would admit to feeling a little fragile and a whole lot sleepy, but she wasn't sick. The one they should be taking care of was her father. The thought of him lying so pale and so gravely ill in the hospital bed was enough to make her suck in her breath and start to sob softly.

"Mr. Josh," Manuela shouted, when Josh had carried Amy halfway up the stairs.

"What is it, Manuela?"

"I say many prayers you come back."

Amy wasn't sure she understood their conversation. The words floated around her like dense fog, so few making sense. She lifted her head and turned to look at the housekeeper, but discovered that Manuela was already rushing toward the kitchen.

Josh entered her bedroom, set her on the edge of her bed and removed her shoes.

"I want a bath," she told him.

He left her sitting on the bed and started running the bathwater, then returned and looked through her chest of drawers until he found a nightgown. He gently led her toward the tub, as if she needed his assistance. Perhaps she did, because the thought of protesting didn't so much as enter her mind.

To her consternation, Amy had to have his help unbuttoning her blouse. She stood lifeless and listless as Josh helped remove her outer clothing.

A few minutes later, Manuela scurried into the bedroom, carrying a tray with her. Frowning and muttering something in her mother tongue, she pushed Josh out of the room and helped Amy finish undressing.

Josh was pacing when Amy reappeared. She had washed and blow-dried her hair, brushed her teeth and changed into the soft flannel gown with a picture of her favorite cartoon cat on the front.

Instantly Josh was at her side, his strong arms encircling her waist.

"Do you feel better?" he inquired gently.

She nodded and noted the way his eyes slid to her lips and lingered there. He wanted to kiss her, she knew from the way his gaze narrowed. Her heart began to hammer when she realized how badly she wanted him to do exactly that. Unhurried, his action filled with purpose, Josh lowered his head.

His mouth was opened over hers. Slowly, as though with heavy reluctance, he slid his hands over her buttocks, molding her tightly to him, tucking her intimately between his legs, which were braced apart.

Amy sighed at the intense pleasure and wrapped her arms around his neck, glorying in the feel of his tongue as it parted her lips and then plunged into her mouth, slowly retreating and then plunging again in a thrilling rhythm, one he had taught her months earlier.

"Amy...no," he groaned as he caressed her derriere as though he couldn't help himself.

She felt the hardening pressure of his manhood pressing against her abdomen and sighed, moving against it, she, too, unable to stop.

"Manuela brought you a bowl of soup," Josh insisted, leading her to the bed.

Like a lost sheep, Amy obediently followed him to where the dinner tray awaited her. Josh sat her down on the edge of the mattress and then placed the table and tray in front of her.

After three bites she was full. Josh coaxed her into taking that many more, but then she protested by closing her eyes and shaking her head.

Josh removed the tray and then pulled back the covers, prepared to tuck her into bed.

"Sleep," he said, leaning over and kissing her once more.

"Are you going away again?"

"No," he whispered, and brushed the hair from her temple.

She caught his hand and brought it to her lips. "Promise me you'll be here when I wake up...I need that, Josh."

"I promise."

Her eyes drifted shut. She heard him move toward the door and she knew that already he was breaking his word. The knowledge was like an unexpected slap in the face and she started to whimper without realizing the sounds were coming from her own throat.

Josh seemed to understand her pain. "I'm taking the tray down to the kitchen. I'll be back in a few minutes, angel, I promise."

Amy didn't believe him, but when she stirred a little while later, she discovered Josh sitting in a chair, leaning forward and intently studying her. His forearms were resting on his knees.

He reached out and ran his finger down the side of her face. "Close your eyes, baby," he urged gently. "You've only been asleep a little while."

Amy scooted as far as she could to the other side of the mattress and patted the empty space at her side, inviting him to join her.

"Amy, no," he said, sucking in his breath. "I can't."

"I need you."

Josh sagged forward, indecision etched in bold lines across his tight features. "Oh, angel, the things you ask of me." He stood and sat next to her. "If I do sleep with you, I'll stay on top of the covers. Understand?"

She thought to protest, but hadn't the strength.

Slowly, Josh lowered his head to the pillow, his eyes gentle on her face, so filled with love and tenderness that her own filled with unexpected tears. One inglorious teardrop rolled from the corner of her eye and over the bridge of her nose, dropping onto the pillow.

Josh caught the second droplet with his index finger, his eyes holding hers.

"Oh, my sweet Amy," he whispered. "My life hasn't been the same from the moment I met you."

She tried to smile, but the result was little more than a pathetic movement of her lips. Closing her eyes, she raised her head just a little, anticipating his kiss.

"So this is how you're going to make me pay for my sins?" he whispered throatily.

Amy's eyes flickered open to discover him studying her with sobering intensity.

"Don't you realize how much I want to make love with you?" he breathed, and his tongue parted her lips for a deep, sensual kiss that left her shaken. She raised her hand and tucked it at the base of his neck, then kissed him back. Although she was starved for his touch, having him in bed with her didn't stir awake sexual sensations, only a deep sense of love and security.

He closed his hand possessively over her hip, dragging her as close as humanly possible against him on the mattress. Even through the unwieldy blankets, Amy could feel the heavy outline of his arousal. He kissed her again, and once more his tongue invaded the recesses of her mouth, tasting and exploring, leaving her breathless and clinging.

Beneath the covers he slid his hand along her midriff until he discovered her breast. Everything seemed to go still as he boldly cupped the soft, enticing fullness.

Amy sighed contentedly as the memory of the wonderful things he had done with her breasts filled her mind. "I want you to taste me," she requested softly. "The way you did before."

Josh's whole body went rigid. "Amy...no."

"Please?" she asked, urging him by taking nibbling kisses at his mouth, biting into his lower lip with her teeth and sucking gently at it the way she wanted him to feast upon her throbbing nipples. To her dismay, she was forced to stop in order to yawn.

"I'll give you anything you want and more," he promised, tucking her head in the crook of his arm. "In a little bit. First close your eyes and rest."

She nodded, barely moving her head. Her lashes drifted downward, and before she knew what was happening, she was stumbling headlong on the path to slumber.

Sometime later Amy stirred. She blinked a couple of times, feeling disoriented and bemused, but when she realized that she was in her own bedroom, she sighed contentedly. The warm, cozy feeling lulled her, and her eyes drifted closed once more. It was then that she felt the large male hand slip from her waist and close over her breast with a familiarity that was as shocking as it was sensual.

With a small cry of dismay, her eyes flew open, and she lifted her head from the thick feather pillow. Josh was asleep at her side, and she pressed her hand over her mouth as the memories rolled into place, forming the missing parts of one gigantic puzzle.

"No," she cried, pushing at his shoulder in a flurry of anger and pain. "How dare you climb into my bed as though you have every right to be here."

Josh's dark eyes flashed open and he instantly frowned, obviously perplexed by her actions. He levered himself up on one elbow, studying her.

"Kindly leave," she muttered between clenched teeth, doing her best to control her outrage.

"Angel Eyes, you invited me to join you, don't you remember?"

"No." She threw back the covers with enough force to pull the sheets free from between the mattress and box springs. To add to her dismay, she discovered that her nightgown had worked its way up her body and was hugging at her waist, exposing a lengthy expanse of leg, thigh and hip. In her rush to escape, she nearly stumbled over her own two feet.

"Will you please get out of my bedroom...or I'll...I'll be forced to phone the police."

"Amy?" Josh sat up and rubbed the sleep from his eyes as though he expected this to be a part of a bad dream. "Be reasonable."

"Leave," she said tersely, throwing open the door to be certain there could be no misunderstanding her request.

"Don't you remember?" he coaxed. "We kissed and held each other and you asked me to—"

"That was obviously a mistake, now get out," she blared, unconsciously using his own phrase. She wasn't in the mood to argue or discuss this—or anything else—rationally. All she knew was that the man she'd been desperately trying to forget was in her bed and looking very much as though he intended to stay right where he was.

Chapter Twelve

A my," Josh said, his voice calm and low, as though he was trying to reason with a deranged woman.

"Out," she cried, squeezing her eyes shut as if that would make him go away.

"All right," he returned, eyeing her dubiously. "If that's what you really want."

The audacity of the man was phenomenal. "It's what I *really* want," she repeated, doing her level best to maintain her dignity.

Josh didn't seem to be in any big rush. He sat on the end of the bed and rubbed his hand down his face before he reached for his shoes. It demanded everything within Amy not to openly admire his brazen good looks. It astonished her that she could have forgotten how easy on the eyes Josh was. Even now, when his expression was impassive, she was struck by the angled lines of his features, as sharp as a blade, more so now as he struggled not to reveal his thoughts.

He stood, but the movement was marked with reluctance. "Can we talk?"

"No," she said, thrusting out her chin defiantly.

"Amy—"

"There's nothing to discuss. I said everything the day you left."

"I was wrong," he admitted softly. "I'd give everything I own if I could turn back time and change what happened that morning. From the bottom of my heart, I'm sorry."

"Of course you were wrong," she cried, fighting the urge to forgive and forget. She couldn't trust Josh anymore. "I knew you'd figure it out sooner or later, but I told you then and I meant it—I don't want you back."

Manuela appeared, breathless from running up the stairs. "Miss Amy... Mr. Josh, hospital is on phone."

In her eagerness to expel Josh from her room, Amy hadn't even heard it ring. "Dear God," she murmured and raced across the room, nearly toppling the telephone from her nightstand in her eagerness.

"Yes?" she cried. "This is Amy Johnson." Nothing but silence greeted her. Frantically, she tried pushing on the phone lever, hoping to get a dial tone.

"I unplugged it," Josh explained and hurriedly replaced the jack in the wall. At her fierce look, he added, "I wanted you to rest undisturbed."

"This is Amy Johnson," she said thickly, her pulse doubling with anxiety and fear.

Immediately the crisp, clear voice of a hospital staff member came on the line. The instant Amy heard that her father was awake and resting comfortably, she slumped onto the mattress and covered her mouth with her hand as tears of relief swamped her eyes.

"Thank you, thank you," she repeated over and over before hanging up the phone.

"Dad's awake...he's apparently doing much better," she told Manuela, wiping the moisture from her face with the side of her hand. "He's asking for me."

"Thank God," Josh whispered.

Amy had forgotten he was there. "Please leave." She cast a pleading glance in Manuela's direction, hoping to gain the housekeeper's support in removing Josh from her bedroom.

"Mr. Chad come to see you," Manuela whispered, as though doing so would prevent Josh from hearing her. "I tell him you asleep."

"Thank you, I'll phone Mr. Morton when I get back from the hospital."

"I also tell him Mr. Josh is back to stay," Manuela said with a triumphant grin.

"If you'll both excuse me," Amy said pointedly, "I'd like to get dressed."

"Of course," Josh answered, as if there had never been a problem. He winked at her on his way out the door, and it was all Amy could do not to throw something after him.

She was trembling when she sat on the edge of her mattress. The emotions battling within her were so potent, she didn't know which one to respond to first. Relief mingled with unbridled joy that her father had taken a decided turn for the better.

The others weren't so easy to identify. Josh was here, making a dramatic entrance into her life when she was too wrapped up in grief and shock to react properly.

Instead, she'd fallen into his arms as though he was Indiana Jones leaping to the rescue, and the memory infuriated her. He could just as easily turn and walk away from her again. She'd suffered through a good deal of heartrending pain to come to that conclusion. And once burned, she knew enough to stay away from the fire.

By the time she had dressed and walked down the stairs, Josh was nowhere to be seen. She searched the living room, then berated herself for looking for him. After all, she had been firm about wanting him to leave. His having left avoided an unpleasant confrontation.

No sooner had the thought passed through her mind when the front door opened and he walked into the house as brazen as could be.

Amy pretended not to see him and stepped into the dining room for a badly needed cup of coffee. She ignored the breakfast Manuela had brought in for her and casually sought her purse and car keys.

"You should eat something," Josh coaxed.

Amy turned and glared at him, but refused to become involved in a dispute over something as nonsensical as scrambled eggs and toast.

"I've got a rental car, if you're ready to go to the hospital now."

"I'll take my own," she informed him briskly.

Josh leaned across the table and reached for the toast on her plate. "Fine, but I assume it's still at the hospital."

Amy closed her eyes in frustration. "I'll take another vehicle then."

"Seems like a waste of gasoline since I'm going that way myself. Besides, how are you going to bring two cars home?"

"All right," she said from between clenched teeth. "Can we leave now?"

"Sure."

Amy told Manuela where she could be reached and walked out to Josh's car, which was parked in front of the house. She climbed inside without waiting for him to open the door for her and stiffly snapped her seat belt into place.

They were in the heavy morning traffic before either spoke again. And it was Josh who ventured into conversation first. "I can help you, Amy, if you'll let me."

"Help me," she repeated with a short, humorless laugh. "How? By slipping into my bed and forcing unwanted attentions on me?" She couldn't believe she had said that. It was so unfair, but she would swallow her tongue before she apologized.

Josh stiffened, but said nothing in his own defense, which made Amy feel even worse. She refused to allow herself to be vulnerable to this man again, least of all now, when she was so terribly alone.

"I'd like to make it up to you for the cruel way I acted," he murmured after a moment.

Her anger stretched like a tightrope between them, and he seemed to be the only one brave enough to bridge the gap.

Amy certainly wasn't. It angered her that Josh thought he could come back as easily as if he'd never been away, apparently expecting to pick up where they'd left off.

"I'd like to talk to your father," he said next.

"No," she said forcefully.

"Amy, there's a good deal you don't know. I could help in ways you don't understand, if you'll let me."

"No, thank you," she returned, her voice hard and inflexible, discounting any appreciation for his offer.

"Oh, Amy, have I hurt you so badly?"

She turned her head and glared out the side window, refusing to answer him. The fifteen-minute ride to the hospital seemed to take an hour. Josh turned into the parking lot, and she hoped he would drop her off at the entrance and drive away. When he pulled into a parking space and turned off the engine, she realized she wasn't going to get her wish.

Biting back a caustic comment, she opened the door and climbed out. Whether he followed her inside or not was his own business, she decided.

She groaned inwardly when the sound of his footsteps echoed behind her on the polished hospital floor. The ride in the elevator was tolerable only because there were several other people with them. Once they arrived on the eighth floor, Amy stopped at the nurses' station and gave her name.

"Ms. Johnson, I was the one who called you this morning," a tall redheaded nurse with a freckled face said. "Your father is looking much better."

"Could I see him, please?"

"Yes, of course, but only for a few minutes."

Amy nodded, understanding all too well how short those moments would be, and followed the nurse into the intensive care unit.

Harold Johnson smiled feebly when she approached his bedside. Her gaze filled with fresh tears that she struggled to hide behind a brilliant smile. His color was better, and although he remained gravely ill, he was awake and able to communicate with her.

"This is a hell of an expensive way to vacation," she said, smiling through the emotion.

"Hi, sweetheart. I'm sorry if I frightened you."

Her fingers gripped his and squeezed tightly. "I'm the one who's sorry... more than you'll ever know. Every time I think about what happened, I blame myself."

A weak shake of his head dismissed her apology. He moistened his mouth and briefly closed his eyes. "I need you to do something."

"Anything."

His fingers tightened around hers, and the pressure was incredibly slight. "It won't be easy, baby... your pride will make it difficult."

"Dad, there isn't anything in this world I wouldn't do for you. Don't waste your strength apologizing. What do you need?"

"Find Joshua Powell for me."

Amy felt as if the floor had started to buckle beneath her feet. She gripped the railing at the side of his bed and dragged in a deep breath. "Josh? Why?"

"He can help."

"Oh, Daddy, I'm sure you mean well, but we don't need Josh." She forced a lightness into her voice, hoping that would reassure him.

"We need him," her father repeated, his voice barely audible.

"Of course, I'm willing to do whatever you want, but we've gotten along fine without him this far," she countered, doing her best to maintain her cheerful facade. Then it dawned on her. "You think *I* need him, don't you? Oh, Dad, I'm stronger than I look. You should know by now that I'm completely over him. Chad and I have a good thing going, and I'd hate to throw a wrench into that relationship by dragging Josh back.''

"Amy," Harold said, his strength depleting quickly. "I'm the one who has to talk to him. Please, do as I ask."

"All right," she agreed, her voice sagging with hesitation.

"Thank you." He closed his eyes then and was almost immediately asleep.

Reluctantly, Amy left his side, perplexed and worried. Josh was pacing the small area designated as a waiting room when she returned.

"How is he?"

"Better."

"Good," Josh said, looking encouraged. His gaze seemed to eat its way through her. "Did you tell him I was here?"

"No."

"You've got to, Amy. I can understand why you'd hesitate, but there are things you don't know or understand. I just might be able to do him some good."

She didn't know what to make of what was happening, but it was clear she was missing something important.

"We've got to talk. Let me buy you breakfast—we can sit down and have a rational discussion."

Amy accepted his invitation with ill grace. "All right, if you insist."

His mouth quirked up at the edges. "I do."

The hospital cafeteria was bustling with people. By the time they had ordered and carried their orange trays through the line, there was a vacant table by the window.

While Amy buttered her English muffin, Josh returned the trays. When he joined her, he seemed unusually quiet for someone who claimed he wanted to talk.

"Well?" she asked with marked impatience. "Say whatever it is that's so important, and be done with it."

"This isn't easy."

"What isn't, telling the truth?" she asked flippantly.

"I never lied to you, Amy. Never," he reinforced. "I'm afraid, however," he said sadly, "that what I'm going to tell you is probably going to hurt you even more."

"Oh? Do you have a wife and family securely tucked away somewhere?"

"You know that isn't true," he answered, his voice slightly elevated with anger. "I'm not a liar or a cheat."

"That's refreshing. What are you?"

"A former business executive. I was CEO for the largest conglomerate in the country for three years."

She raised her eyebrows, unimpressed. That he should mislead her about something like this didn't shock her. He had misrepresented himself before, and another violation of trust wasn't going to prejudice her one way or the other. "And I thought you were into oil. Fancy that."

"I was, or have been for the past several years. I left the company."

"Why?" She really didn't care, but if he was willing to tell her, then she would admit to being semicurious as to the reason he found this admission to be such a traumatic one.

"That's not important," he said forcefully. "What is vital now is that I might be able to help your father save his company. These are dangerous times for him."

"He's not going to lose it," she returned confidently.

"Amy, I don't know how much you're aware of what's going on, but Johnson Industries is a prime candidate for a hostile takeover by any number of corporate raiders."

"I know that. But we've got the best minds in the country dealing with his finances. We don't need you."

"I've been there, I know how best to handle this type of situation."

She sighed expressively, giving the impression that she was bored with this whole conversation, which wasn't entirely false. "Personally, I think it's supremely arrogant of you to think you could waltz your way into my father's business and claim to be the cure of all our ills."

"Amy, please," he said, clearly growing frustrated with her.

Actually she didn't blame him. She wasn't making this easy for a reason. There were too many negative emotions tied to Josh for her to blithely accept his offer of assistance.

"The next time you see Harold, ask him about me," he suggested.

The mention of her father tightened Amy's stomach. It was apparent that Harold already knew, otherwise he wouldn't have pleaded with her to find Josh. Nor would he have offered Josh a position with the firm. But they both had kept Josh's past a secret from her. The pain of their deception cut deep and sharp. Her father she could forgive. But Josh had already hurt her so intensely that another wound inflicted upon one still open and raw only increased her emotional anguish.

Valiantly, she struggled to disguise it. What little appetite she possessed vanished. She pushed her muffin aside and checked her watch, pretending to be surprised by the time. With a flippant air, she excused herself and hurried from the cafeteria.

Blindly, she stumbled into the ladies' room and braced her trembling hands against the sink as she sucked in deep breaths in an effort to control the pain. The last thing she wanted was for Josh to know he still had the power to hurt her. The sense of betrayal by the two men she'd loved the most in her life grew sharper with every breath.

Running the water, Amy splashed her face and dried it with the rough paper towel. When she'd composed herself, she squared her shoulders and walked out of the room, intent on returning to the intensive care unit.

She stopped abruptly in the hallway when she noticed that Josh was leaning against the wall waiting for her. Her facade was paper-thin, and he was the last person she was ready to deal with at the moment.

"I suppose I should mention that my father asked me to find you when I spoke to him this morning," she said when she could talk.

Josh's dark eyes flickered with surprise and then relief. "Good."

"You might as well go to him now."

"No," he said firmly, and shook his head. "We need to clear the air between us first."

"That's not necessary," she returned flatly. "There isn't anything I want to say to you. Or hear from you. Or have to do with you."

He nodded and tucked his hands in his pants pockets as if he had to do something in order not to reach out to her. "I can understand that, but I can't accept it." He paused as two orderlies walked past them on their way into the cafeteria. "Perhaps now isn't the best time, but at least believe me when I say I love you."

Amy pretended to yawn.

Josh's eyes narrowed and his mouth thinned. "You're not fooling me, Amy, I know you feel the same thing for me."

"It wouldn't matter if I did," she answered calmly. "What I feel—or don't feel for you—doesn't change a thing. If you and my father believe you can help the company, then more power to you. If you're looking for my blessing, then you've got it. I'd bargain with the devil himself if it would help my father. Do what you need to do, then kindly get out of my life."

Josh flinched as if she had struck him.

Amy didn't understand why he should be so shocked. "How many times do I have to tell you to leave me alone before you believe me?"

"Amy." He gripped her shoulders, the pressure hard and painful as he stared into her eyes. "Dear God, did I do this to you?"

"If anyone is at fault, I am. I fell in love with the wrong man, but I've learned my lesson," she told him bitterly. Boldly, she met his stare, but the hurt and doubt in his dark eyes were nearly her undoing. Without another word, she freed herself from his grasp and headed toward the elevator.

Josh followed her, and they rode up to the eighth floor in an uncomfortable silence. She approached the nurses' station and explained that her father had requested to talk to Josh.

She had turned away, prepared to leave the hospital, when the elevator doors opened and Chad Morton stepped out.

"Amy," he cried, as if he expected her to vanish into thin air before he reached her. "I've been trying to see you for two days."

"I'm sorry," she said, accepting his warm embrace.

"I stopped off at the hospital yesterday, but I was told you'd gone home. When I drove to the house, Manuela explained that you were asleep."

"Yes, I...I was exhausted. In fact, I wasn't myself," she said pointedly for Josh's benefit.

"With little wonder. You'd been here every minute since your father's heart attack. If you hadn't gone home, I would have taken you there myself."

Amy could feel Josh's stare penetrate her shoulder blades, but she ignored him. "I was just leaving," she explained. "I thought I'd check in at the office this morning."

Chad's frown darkened his face. "I...I don't think that would be a good idea."

"Why not?"

It was clear that Chad was uncomfortable. His gaze shifted to the floor, and he buried his hands in his pockets. "The office is a madhouse with the news and...and, well, frankly, there's a good deal of speculation going around—"

"Speculation?" she asked. "About what?"

"The takeover."

"What are you talking about?" She'd known that their situation was a prime one for a hostile takeover—in theory at least—but the reality of it caused her face to pale.

Chad looked as though he would give his right arm not be be the one to tell her this. He hesitated and drew in a breath. "Johnson shares had gone up three dollars by the time Wall Street closed yesterday. Benson's moved in."

George Benson was a well-known corporate raider, the worst of the lot, from what little Amy knew. His reputation was that of a greedy, harsh man who bought out companies and then proceeded to bleed them dry with little or no compassion.

Amy closed her eyes for a moment, trying to maintain a modicum of control. "Whatever you do, you mustn't tell my father any of this."

"He already knows," Josh said starkly from behind her. "Otherwise, he wouldn't have asked for me."

Chad's troubled gaze narrowed as it swung to Josh. "Who is this?" he asked Amy.

Purposely, she turned and stared at Josh. "A friend of my father's." With that she turned and walked away.

Josh lost track of time. He and Lloyd Dickins had pored over the company's financial records until they were both seeing double. They needed a good deal of money, and they needed it fast. George Benson had seen to it that they were unable to borrow the necessary funds, and he had also managed to close off the means of selling some collateral, even if it meant at a loss. Every corner he turned, Josh was confronted by the financial giant who loomed over Johnson Industries like black death. Harold Johnson's company was a fat plum, and Benson wasn't about to let this one fall through his greedy little fingers.

"Are we going to be able to do it?" Lloyd Dickins asked, eyeing Josh speculatively.

Josh leaned back in his chair, pinched the bridge of his nose and sadly shook his head. "I don't see how."

"There's got to be some way."

"Everything we've tried hasn't done a damn bit of good."

"Who does George Benson think he is, anyway?" Lloyd flared. "God?"

"At the moment, he's got us down with our hands tied behind our backs," Josh admitted reluctantly. The pencil he was holding snapped in half. He hadn't realized his hold had been so tight.

"The meeting of the board of directors is Friday. We're going to have to come up with some answers by then."

"We will," but the confidence in Josh's voice sounded shaky at best. He had run out of suggestions. Years before, his ideas had been considered revolutionary. He never *had* been one to move with the crowd, nor did he base his decisions on what everyone else was doing around him. He had discovered early on that if he started looking to his colleagues before making a move he would surrender his leading edge to his business peers. That realization had carried him far. But he had been out of the scene for too many years. His instincts had been blunted, his mind baffled by the changes. Yet he had loved every minute of this. It was as if he was playing a good game of chess—only this time the stakes were higher than anything he had ever wagered. He couldn't lose.

"I think I'll go home and sleep on it," Lloyd murmured, yawning loudly. "I'm so rummy now I can't think straight."

"Go ahead. I'll look over these figures one more time and see what I can come up with."

Lloyd nodded. "I'll see you in the morning." He hesitated, then chuckled, the sound rusty and discordant. "Hell, it *is* morning. Before much longer this place is going to be hopping, but as long as it isn't with Benson's people, I'll be content."

Josh grinned, but the ability to laugh had left him several hours ago. A feeling of impending doom was pounding at him like a prizefighter's fist, each blow driving him farther and farther until his back was pressed against the wall.

There had to be a way...for Amy and her father's sake, he needed to find one. With a determination born of desperation, he went over the numbers one last time.

"What are you doing here?"

Amy's voice cracked against his ears like a horsewhip. His eyes flew open, and he blinked several times against the bright light. He must have dozed off, he realized. With his elbows braced against the table, he rubbed the sleep from his face. "What time is it?"

"Almost seven."

"Isn't it a little early for you?" he asked, checking his watch, blinking until his eyes focused on the dial.

"I...I had something I needed to check on. You look absolutely terrible," she said, sounding very much like a prim schoolteacher taking a student to task. "You'd better go to your hotel and get some sleep before you pass out."

"I will in a minute," Josh answered, hiding a smile. Her concern was the first indication she still loved him that she'd shown since the morning she awoke with him in her bed. That had been...what? Two weeks ago? The days had merged in his mind, and he wasn't entirely certain of the date even now.

"Josh, you're going to make yourself sick."

"Would you care?"

"No...but it would make my father feel guilty when I tell him, and he's got enough to worry about."

"Speaking of Harold, how's he doing?"

"Much better."

"Good."

Amy remained on the other side of the room. Josh gestured toward the empty chair beside him. "Sit down and talk to me a minute while I gather my wits."

"Your wits are gathered enough."

"Come on, Amy, I'm not the enemy."

Her returning look said she disagreed.

"All right," he said, standing, "walk me to the elevator then."

"I'm not sure I should...you know the way. What do you need me for?" She held herself stiffly, as far on the other side of the office as she could get and still be in the same room with him.

"Moral support. I'm exhausted and hungry and too tired to argue. Besides, I have a meeting at nine. It's hardly worth going to the hotel."

"My dad has a sofa in his office...you could rest there for an hour or so," she said, watching him closely.

Josh hesitated, thinking he'd much rather spend the time holding and kissing her. "I could," he agreed. "But I wouldn't rest well alone." Boldly his eyes held hers. "The fact is, I need you to nourish me."

"You can forget it, Joshua Powell," she said heatedly. She was blushing, very prettily, too, as she turned and walked out of Lloyd Dickins's office.

Josh followed her. When she stepped into her father's office, he dutifully closed the door.

"I...think there's a blanket around here somewhere." She walked into a huge closet that contained supplies. Josh went in after her, resisting the temptation to slip his arms around her and drag her against him.

"Here's one," she said and when she turned around he was directly behind her, blocking any way of escape. Her startled eyes clashed with his. Josh loved her all the more as she drew herself up to her full height and set her chin at a proud, haughty angle. "Kindly let me go."

"I can't."

"Why not?" she demanded.

"Because there's something else I need far more than sleep."

She braced one hand against her hip, prepared to do battle. Only Josh didn't want to fight. Arguing was the last thing on his mind.

"What do you want, Joshua?" she asked.

"I already told you. We should start with a kiss, though, don't you think?"

Astonished, she glared at him. "You've got to be out of your mind if you think I'm going to let you treat me as though I was some brainless—"

Josh had no intention of listening to her tirade. Without waiting for her to pause to breathe, he clasped his hands around her waist and dragged her against his chest. She opened her mouth in outrage, and Josh took instant advantage by plunging his tongue inside.

Amy tried to resist him. Josh felt her fingernails curl into the material of his shirt as if she intended to push him away, but whatever her intent had been, she abruptly changed her mind. She may have objected to his touching her, but before she could stop herself, her tongue was mating with his and small moaning sounds were coming from her throat. Or was he the one making the noise?

"Oh...oh..."

At the startled gasp, Josh broke off the kiss and shielded Amy from probing eyes.

Ms. Wetherell, Harold Johnson's secretary, was standing in the office, looking so pale it was a wonder that she didn't keel over in a dead faint.

Chapter Thirteen

Matters weren't looking good for Johnson Industries. Amy didn't need to attend the long series of meetings with Josh and the department executives to know that. The gloomy looks of those around her told her everything she needed to know. Lloyd Dickins, usually so professional, had been short-tempered all week, snapping at everyone close to him. His movements were sluggish, as if he dreaded each day, so unlike the vivacious man whose company she'd come to enjoy.

Twice in the past two weeks, Amy had found Ms. Wetherell dabbing at her eyes with a spotless lace hankie. The grandmotherly woman who'd served her father for years seemed older and less like a dragon than ever.

Amy sincerely doubted that Josh had slept more than a handful of hours all week. For that matter, she hadn't either. In the evenings when she left the office, she headed directly for the hospital. Josh had made several visits there himself once her father was moved out of the intensive care unit, but the older man always seemed cheered after Josh had stopped by. Amy knew Josh wasn't telling Harold the whole truth, but, despite their differences, she approved and didn't intervene.

For her part, Amy had avoided being alone with Josh since that one incident when Ms. Wetherell had discovered them. She had learned early on that she couldn't trust Josh, but he taught her a second more painful lesson—*she couldn't trust herself around him*. Two seconds in his arms and all her resolve disappeared. Even now, days later, her face heated at the memory of the way she had opened to his impudent kisses.

"How's he doing?"

Amy straightened in her chair beside her father's hospital bed. Josh, the very object of her musings, entered the darkened room. "Fine. I think."

"He's sleeping?"

"Yes."

Josh claimed the chair next to her and rubbed a hand down his face as if to disguise the lines of worry, but he wasn't fooling her. Just seeing him caused her heart to throb with concern. He looked terrible. Sighing inwardly, Amy guessed that she probably wasn't in much better shape herself.

"When was the last time you had a decent night's sleep?" she couldn't help asking.

He tried to reassure her with a smile, but failed. "About the same time you did. Dammit, Amy, it doesn't look good. You know as well as I do how poorly that meeting went with the board of directors this afternoon. We're fighting even more of an uphill battle than we first realized. Half are in favor of selling out now, thinking we might get a better price, and no one's willing to speculate what Benson will be offering next week.''

"We . . . we can't let my father know."

Josh shrugged. "I don't know how we can keep it from him. He's too smart not to have figured it out. We've done everything we can to hide it, but I'm sure he knows."

Amy nodded, accepting the truth of Josh's statement. She was all too aware of the consequences of the takeover. It would kill her father as surely if George Benson was to shoot him through the heart. Johnson Industries was the blood that flowed through her father's veins. Without the business, his life would lack purpose and direction.

Josh must have read her thoughts. His hand reached for hers, and he squeezed her fingers reassuringly. "It's going to work out," he told her. "Don't worry."

"It looks like you're doing enough of that for the both of us."

He tried smiling again, this time succeeding. "There's too much at stake to give up. If I lose this company," he said, his eyes holding hers, "I lose you."

Amy's gaze fell to her lap as his words circled her mind like a lariat around the head of a steer. "You lost me a long time ago."

The air between them seemed to crackle with electricity. Amy could almost taste his defeat. So much was already riding on Josh's shoulders without her adding her head as a prize. Whatever happened happened. What was between them had nothing to do with that.

"I can't accept that."

"Maybe you should."

"You can't fool me, Amy. You love me."

"I did once," she admitted reluctantly, "but, as you so often had told me in the past, that was a mistake. Chad and I—"

"Chad!" He spat out the name as if it were a piece of spoiled meat. "You can't honestly expect me to believe you're in love with that Milquetoast."

A tense moment passed before she spoke again. "I think we'd best end this conversation before we both lose our tempers."

"No," he jeered. "We're going to have this out right now. I'm through playing games."

"Talk this out? Here and now?" she flared. "I refuse to discuss anything of importance with you in my father's hospital room."

"Fine. We'll leave."

"Fine," she countered, nearly leaping to her feet in her eagerness. She felt a little like a boxer jumping out from his corner at the beginning of a new round. Every minute she was with Joshua, he infuriated her more.

At a crisp pace, she followed him out of the hospital to the parking lot. "Where are we going?" she demanded, when he calmly unlocked the passenger side of his car door.

"Where do you suggest?" he asked, as casually as if he was seeking her preference for a restaurant.

"I couldn't care less." His collected manner only served to irritate her all the more. The least he could do was reveal a little emotion. For her part, she was brimming with it. It was all she could do not to throw her purse to the ground and go at him with both fists. The amount of emotion churning inside her was a shock.

"All right then, *I'll* decide." He motioned toward the open car door. "Get in."

"Not until I know where we're headed."

"I don't plan on kidnapping you."

"Where are we going?" she demanded a second time, certain her eyes must be sparking with outrage and fury.

"My hotel room."

Amy slapped her hands against her thighs. "Oh, brother," she cried. "Honestly, Josh, do I look that stupid? I simply can't believe you! There is no way in hell that I'd go to a hotel room with you."

He stood on the driver's side, the open door between them. "Why not?" he asked.

"You . . . you're planning to seduce me."

"Would I succeed?"

"Not likely."

Unconcerned, Josh shrugged. "Then what's the problem?"

"I . . ." She couldn't very well admit that he was too damn tempting for her own good.

"We're closer to my hotel than your house, and at least there we'll be afforded some privacy. I can't speak for you, but personally, I'd prefer to discuss this in a rational manner without half of Seattle listening in."

He had her there. Talk about taking the wind out of her sails! "All right, then, but I'd rather drive there in my own car."

"Fine." He climbed inside his vehicle, leaned across the plush interior and closed the passenger door, which he had opened seconds earlier for her.

The ride to the hotel took only a few minutes. There was a minor problem with parking, which was probably the reason Josh had suggested she ride with him. Since there wasn't any space on the street, she found a lot, paid the attendant and then met Josh in the lobby.

"Are you hungry?"

She was, but unwilling to admit it. The hotel was the same one where he had been staying when she had first met him. The realization did little to settle her taut nerves. "No."

"If you don't object, I'll order something from room service."

"Fine."

The air between them during the elevator ride was still and ominous, like the quiet before a tornado touches down.

Josh had his key ready by the time they reached his room. He unlocked the door and opened it for her to precede him. She stopped abruptly when she realized that even the *room* was identical to the one he'd had months earlier. How differently she'd felt about him then. Even then she'd been in love with him.

And now... well, now, she'd learned so many things. But most of those lessons had been painful. She'd come a long way from the naive college graduate she'd been then. Most of her maturing had come as a result of her relationship with Josh.

"This is the same room you had before," she said, without realizing she'd verbalized her thought.

"It looks the same, but I'm on a different floor," Josh agreed absentmindedly. He reached for the room service menu and scanned its listings before heading toward the phone. "Are you sure I can't change your mind?"

"I'm sure." Her stomach growled in angry protest to the lie. Amy gave a brilliant performance of pretending the noise had come from someone other than herself.

Josh ordered what seemed like an exorbitant amount of food and then turned toward her. "All right, let's get this over with."

"Right," she said, squaring her shoulders for the coming confrontation.

"Sit down." He motioned toward a chair that was angled in front of the window.

"If you don't mind, I'd like to stand."

"Fine." He claimed the chair for himself.

Amy had thought standing would give her an advantage. Not so. She felt even more intimidated by Josh than at any time in recent memory. Garnering what she could of her emotional fortitude, she squared her shoulders and met his look head on, asking no quarter and giving none herself.

"You wanted to say something to me," she prompted, when he didn't immediately pick up the conversation.

"Yes," Josh reiterated, looking composed and not the least bit irritated. "I don't want you seeing Chad Milquetoast again."

Amy snickered at the colossal nerve of the man. "You and what army are going to stop me?"

"I won't need an army. You're making a fool of him and an even bigger one of yourself. I love you, and you love me, and frankly, I'm tired of having you use Chad Morton as an excuse every time we meet."

"I was hoping you'd get the message," she said, crossing her arms over her waist. "As for this business of my still loving you," she said, forcing a soft laugh, "any feeling I have for you died ages ago."

"Don't lie, Amy, you do a damn poor job of it. You always have."

"Not this time," she told him flatly. "In fact, I can remember the precise moment I stopped loving you, Joshua Powell. It happened when you stepped inside a taxi that was parked outside my home. I . . . I stood there and watched as you drove away, and I swore to myself that I'd never allow a man to hurt me like that again."

Josh briefly closed his eyes and lowered his head. "Leaving you that day was the most difficult thing I'd ever done in my life, Amy. I said before that I'd give anything for it never to have happened. Unfortunately, it did."

"Do you honestly believe that a little contrition is going to change everything?"

Josh leaned back in the chair, and his shoulders sagged with fatigue. "I was hoping it would be a start."

"A few regrets aren't enough," she cried, and to her horror, she felt the tears stinging in the back of her eyes. Before they brimmed and Josh had a chance to see them, she turned and walked away from him.

"What do you want?" he demanded. "Blood?"

"Yes," she cried. "Much more than that . . . I want you out of my life. You . . . you seem to think that . . . that if you're able to help my father, that's going to wipe out everything that's happened before and that . . . I'll be willing to let bygones be bygones and we can marry and have two point five children and live happily ever after."

"Amy . . ."

"No, Josh," she cried, and turned around, stretching her arm out in front of her in an effort to ward him off. "I refuse to be some prize you're going to collect once this craziness with George Benson passes and my father recovers."

"It's not that."

"Then what is it?"

"I love you."

"That's not enough," she cried. "And as for my not seeing Chad Morton again...there's something you should know. I...plan on marrying Chad. He hasn't asked me yet, but he will, and when he does, I'll gladly accept his proposal."

"You don't love Chad," Josh cried, leaping from his chair. "I can't believe you'd do anything so stupid!"

"I may not love Chad the way I love—used to love you, but at least if he ever walks out on me it won't hurt nearly as badly. But then, Chad never would leave me— not the way you did at any rate."

"Amy, don't do anything crazy. Please, Angel Eyes, you'd be ruining our lives."

"Chad's wonderful to me."

Momentarily, Josh closed his eyes. "Give me a chance to make everything up to you."

"No." She shook her head wildly, backing away from him, taking tiny steps as he advanced toward her. "Chad's kindhearted and good."

"He'd bore you out of your mind in two weeks."

"He's honorable and gentle," she continued, holding his gaze.

"But what kind of lover would he be?"

Amy's shoulders sagged with defeat. Chad's kisses left her cold. Josh must have known it. A spark of triumph flashed from his eyes when she didn't immediately respond to his taunt.

"Answer me," he demanded, his eyes brightening.

Amy had backed away from him as far as she could. Her back was pressed to the wall.

"When Chad touches you, what do you feel?"

The lie died on the end of her tongue. She could shout that she came alive in Chad Morton's arms, insist that he was an enviable lover, but it would do little good. Josh would recognize the lie and make her suffer for it.

Slowly, almost without her being aware of it, Josh lifted his hand and ran his fingertips down the side of her face. Her nerves sprang to life at his feather-light stroke, and she sharply inhaled her breath, unprepared for the onslaught of sensation his touch aroused.

"Does your Mr. BMW make you feel anything close to this?" he asked, his voice hushed and ultra-seductive.

It was a strain to keep from closing her eyes and giving in to the sensual awareness Josh brought to life within her. She raised her hands, prepared to push him away, but the instant they came into contact with the hard, muscular planes of his chest, they lost their purpose.

"I don't feel anything. Kindly take your hands off me."

Josh chuckled softly. "I'm not touching you, angel, you're the one with your hands on me. Oh, baby," he groaned, his amusement weaving its way through his words. "You put up such a fierce battle."

Mortified, Amy dropped her hands, but not before Josh flattened his against the wall and trapped her there, using his body to hold her in check.

Amy's immediate reaction was to struggle, pound his chest and demand that he release her. But the wild, almost primitive look in his eyes dragged all the denial out of her. His pulse throbbed at the base of his throat like a drum, hammering out her fate. He held himself almost completely rigid, but Amy could feel the entire length of him pulsating with tension.

It came to her then that if she didn't do something to stop him, he was going to make love with her. The taste of bitter defeat filled her throat. Once he became her lover, she would never be able to send him away.

Her breath clogged her throat and she bucked against him, but the action only alerted her to the fact that he was already unbelievably aroused. Her eyes flew to his face, and he smiled.

"That's right, angel," he urged in a deep whisper. "Feel me. Move against me. Let me know how much you want me, too."

"No," she murmured, but her protest was feeble.

He kissed her then. Slow and deep, as if they had all the time in the world. Against every dictate of her will, blistering excitement rushed through her and she moaned. Her small cry seemed to please him, and he kissed her again, and when his tongue found hers, she welcomed it, wanting to weep with abject frustration at the treachery of her body.

His hands were at the front of her blouse, unfastening each button with an urgency that should have frightened her, but didn't. Once he'd succeeded, he stripped the jacket from her shoulders. Her silk blouse and her bra followed.

Knowing his intention, Amy made one final plea. "Josh . . . no . . . please."

His shoulders and chest lifted with a sharp intake of breath.

He hadn't so much as touched her bare breasts and already they were tightening, her nipples so puckered they throbbed painfully.

He bent and gently wet each one in turn, rolling his tongue around the pebbled hardness, sucking lightly.

When they were moist and shining, he slid his face from one to the other, lapping and sucking alternately until it was all Amy could do not to cry out and beg him to stop. Only it would have been another lie. The last thing she wanted him to do was cease his glorious ministrations. She longed for more and more and more.

She felt his hands gather her skirt around her waist, then lower her panty hose halfway to her knees. This new invasion should have been enough for her to realize that if they didn't put an end to this now, it would be too late. But reason had been lost to her the moment he kissed her.

He slid his hands over her naked buttocks, caressing them, lifting her against his arousal so there could be no doubt in her mind what he intended. He opened her legs with his palms, then with one hand he cupped her, delving one finger between the soft folds of her womanhood.

Amy gasped, and her eyes flew open. She pressed her head against the wall and dug her nails viciously into his shoulders. Then, unable to stop herself, she started to writhe against his finger until the spasms of intense pleasure overtook her.

She bit into her lower lip, not able to believe what Josh was doing to her, the way he was touching her, the way he continued to rub her again and again. Her head spun, and she tossed it from side to side against the wall, lost in the incredible feeling. Still he wasn't satisfied.

"Again, angel," he urged.

"No," she moaned. "I can't bear it."

"You can."

He stroked her into delirium and then he swallowed her cries of ecstasy with his mouth. Her hips bucked against him until she was consumed a second time by spasms of such keen gratification that tears fell from her eyes, wetting her cheeks and falling onto her breasts. Josh followed the path of her teardrops and licked them from her nipples with obvious delight. Before she could control her hands, they were digging in his hair while he took his nourishment from her.

The polite knock against the door startled them both. Josh tensed and sweat beaded his fervent face. He kissed her hard and moved between her legs, spreading them to make room for her to nestle his pulsating hardness.

"Josh," she moaned, "the door...someone's at the door."

"This time we finish," he growled.

The knock came a second time. "Room service," the male voice boomed from the other side. "I have your order."

"Please," she begged, tears filling her eyes. "Let me go."

Reluctantly, he released her, and after jerking up her panty hose, Amy fled into the bathroom, taking her clothes with her. From inside she could hear Josh dealing with the man who delivered the meal. She was dressing as fast as she could, stuffing her blouse into the waistband of her skirt and running her splayed fingers through her mussed hair.

"Amy. He's gone."

Leaning against the sink, she splashed cold water on her face and tried to interject sound reason into her badly shaken composure.

When she left the bathroom, it demanded every ounce of inner strength she possessed. As she knew he would be, Josh was waiting for her, prepared to continue as if nothing had happened.

She raised her shoulders and focused her gaze just past him, on the picture that hung over the king-size bed. "You proved your point," she said, shocked by how incredibly shaky her voice sounded.

"I hope to God that's true. You're going to marry me, Amy."

"No," she said flatly. "Just because I respond to you physically...doesn't mean I love you, or that I'm willing to trust you with my heart. Not again, Josh, never again."

Before he could say or do anything that would change her mind, she grabbed her purse and left the room.

Amy spent the next four days with her father, purposefully avoiding Josh. In light of what had happened in his hotel room, she didn't know if she would ever be able to look him in the eye again. If the hotel staff hadn't decided to deliver his meal when they had, there was no telling how far their lovemaking would have progressed.

No, she reluctantly amended, she *did* know where it would have ended. With her in his bed, her eyes filled with adoration, her body sated with his lovemaking. Without question, she would have handed him her heart and her life and anything else he demanded.

"You haven't been yourself in days," Chad complained over lunch. "Is there anything I can do?"

No matter what Josh believed about the other man, Chad had been wonderful. He'd anticipated her every need. Amy didn't so much as have to ask. More often than not, he arrived at the hospital, insisting that he was taking her to lunch, or to dinner, or simply out for a breath of fresh air.

Rarely did he stay and talk to her father, and for his part, Harold Johnson didn't have much to say to the other man, either.

"How's everything at the office?" she asked, recognizing that she was really inquiring about Josh and angry with herself for needing to know.

"Not good," Chad admitted, dipping his fork into his avocado and alfalfa-sprout salad. "Several of the staff have turned in their resignations, wanting to find other positions while they can."

"Already?" Amy was alarmed, fearing her father's reaction to the news. She hoped Josh would shield him from most of the unpleasantness.

"When Powell left, most everyone realized it was a lost cause. I want you to know that I'll be here for however long you and your father need me."

"Josh left?" Amy cried, before she could school her reaction. A numb pain worked its way out from her heart, rippling over her abdomen. The paralyzing agony edged its way down her arms and legs until it was nearly impossible to breathe or move to function normally.

"He moved out yesterday," Chad added conversationally. "I'm surprised your father didn't say anything."

"Yes," she murmured, lowering her gaze. For several moments it was all she could do to keep from breaking down into bitter tears.

"Amy, are you all right?"

"No... I've got a terrible headache." She pressed her fingertips to her temple and offered him a smile.

"Let me take you home."

"No," she said, lightly shaking her head. "If you could just take me back to the hospital. I . . . my car is there."

"Of course."

An entire lifetime passed before Amy could leave the restaurant. On the ride to the hospital, she realized how subdued her father had been for the past twenty-four hours. Although his recovery was progressing at a fast pace, he seemed lethargic and listless that morning, but Amy had been too wrapped up in her own problems to probe. Now it all made sense.

When the going got tough, Josh packed his bags and walked out of their lives. He hadn't even bothered to say goodbye—at least not to her. Apparently, he hadn't been able to face her, and with little wonder. Harold had needed him, even if she didn't. But none of that had mattered to Josh. He had turned his back on them and their problems and simply walked away.

"Why didn't you tell me?" Amy demanded of her father the moment they were alone. Hot tears streaked her face. "Josh is gone."

"I thought you knew."

"No." She wiped away the moisture that smeared her cheeks and took in a calming breath before forcing a brave front for her father's sake. "He didn't say a word to me."

"He'll be back," her father assured her, gently patting her hand. "Don't be angry with him, sweetheart, he did everything he could."

"I don't care if he ever comes back," she cried, unable to hold in the bitterness. "I never want to see him again. Ever."

"Amy . . ."

"I'll be married to Chad before Josh returns, I swear I will. I detest the man, I swear I hate him with everything that's in me." She had yet to recover from the first time he had deserted her, and then in their greatest hour of need, he had done it a second time. If her father lost Johnson Industries, and in all likelihood he would, then Amy would know exactly who to blame.

"There's nothing left that he could do," her father reasoned. "I don't blame him. He tried everything within his power to turn the tide, but it was too late. I should have realized it long before now—I was asking the impossible. Josh knew it, and still he tried to find a way out."

"But what about the company?"

"All is lost now, and there's nothing we can do but accept it."

Amy buried her face in her hands.

"We'll recover," her father said, and his voice cracked. He struggled for a moment to compose himself before he spoke again. "I may be down, but I'm not out."

"Oh, Daddy." She hugged him close, offering what comfort she could, but it was damn little when her own heart was crippled with the pain of Josh's desertion.

Chapter Fourteen

By the weekend, Amy came to believe in miracles. Knowing that her father was about to lose the conglomerate he had invested his entire life building, she had been prepared for the worst. What happened was something that only happened to those who believe in fairy tales and Santa Claus. At the eleventh hour, her father sold a small subsidiary company that he had purchased several years earlier. The company, specializing in plastics, had been an albatross and a money loser, but an unexpected bid had come in, offering an inflated price. Her father and the corporate attorneys leaped at the opportunity, signing quickly. Immediately afterward, Johnson Industries was able to pay off its bondholders, all within hours of its deadline. By the narrowest of margins, the company had been able to fend off George Benson and his takeover schemes.

The following week, her father was like a young man again. His spirits were so high that his doctors decided he could be released from the hospital the coming Friday.

"Good morning, beautiful," Harold greeted his daughter when she stopped in to see him on her way to work Monday morning. "It's a beautiful day, isn't it, sweetheart?"

Not as far as Amy was concerned. Naturally, she was pleased with the way matters had turned out for her father, but everything else in her life had taken a sharp downward twist.

Carefully, she had placed a shield around her heart, thinking that would protect her from Josh and anything he might say or do. But she had been wrong. Having him desert her and her father when they needed him most hurt more the second time than it had the first.

Amy found it a constant struggle not to break down and cry. She could weep at the most nonsensical matters. A romantic television commercial produced tears, as did a sad newspaper article or having to wait extra long in traffic. She could be standing in a grocery aisle and find a sudden, unexplainable urge to cry.

"It's rainy, cold and the weatherman said it might snow," she responded to her father's comment about it being a beautiful day, doing her best to maintain a cheerful facade and failing miserably.

"Amy?" Her father's soft blue eyes questioned her. "Do you want to talk about it?"

"No," she responded forcefully. It wouldn't do the least bit of good. Josh was out of their lives, and she couldn't be happier or more sad.

"Is it about Josh?"

Her jaw tightened so hard her back teeth ached. "What possible reason would I have to feel upset about Joshua Powell?" she asked, making his question sound almost comical.

"You love him, sweetheart."

"I may have at one time, but it's over. Lately...I think I could hate him." Those nonsensical tears she had been experiencing during the past two weeks rushed to the corners of her eyes like water spilling over a top-full barrel. Once more, she struggled to disguise them.

Narrowing his gaze, Harold Johnson motioned toward the chair. "Sit down, sweetheart, there's a story I want to tell you."

Instead, Amy walked to the window, her arms cradling her waist. "I've got to get to work. Perhaps another time."

"Nothing is more important than this tale. Now, sit down and don't argue with me. Don't you realize, I've got a bad heart?"

"Oh, Dad." She found herself chuckling.

"Sit." Once more he pointed toward the chair.

Amy did as he asked, bemused by his attitude.

"This story starts out several years back..."

"Is this a once-upon-a-time tale?"

"Hush," her father reprimanded. "Just listen. You can ask all the questions you want later."

"All right, all right," she said with ill grace.

"Okay, now where was I?" he mumbled, and stroked his chin while he apparently gathered his thoughts. "Ah, yes, I'd only gotten started.

"This is the story of a young man who graduated with top honors at a major university. He revealed an extraordinary talent for business, and word of him spread even before he'd received his MBA. I suspect he came by this naturally, since his own father was a well-known stockbroker. At any rate, this young man's ideas were revolutionary, but by God, he had a golden touch. Several corporations wanted him for their CEO. Before long he could name his own terms, and he did.''

"Dad?'' Amy had no idea where this story was leading, but she really didn't want to sit and listen to him ramble on about someone she wasn't even sure she knew. And if this was about Josh, she would rather not hear it. It couldn't change anything.

"Hush and listen," her father admonished. "This young man and his father were apparently very close and had been for years. To be frank, the father had something of a reputation for doing things just a tad shady. Nothing illegal, don't misunderstand me, but he took unnecessary risks. I sincerely doubt that the son was fully aware of this, although he must have guessed some of it was true. The son, however, defended his father at every turn.''

Amy glanced at her watch, hoping her father got her message. If he did, it apparently didn't faze him.

"It seems that the son often sought his father's advice. I suppose this was only natural, being that they were close. By this time, the son was head of a major conglomerate, and if I said the name you'd recognize it immediately.''

Amy yawned, wanting her father to arrive at the point of this long, rambling fable.

"No one is exactly certain what happened, but the conglomerate decided to sell off several of its smaller companies. The father, who you remember was a stockbroker, apparently got wind of the sale from the son and with such valuable inside information, made a killing in the market."

"But that's—"

"Unethical and illegal. What happened between the father and son afterward is anyone's guess. I suspect they parted ways over this issue. Whatever happened isn't my business, but I'm willing to speculate that there was no love lost between the two men in the aftermath of this scandal. The son resigned his position and disappeared for years."

"Can you blame him?"

"No," her father replied, his look thoughtful. "Although it was a terrible waste of talent. Few people even knew what had happened, but apparently he felt his credibility had been weakened. His faith in his father had been destroyed, no doubt, and that blow was the most crushing. My feeling is that he'd lived with the negative effects of having money for so many years that all he wanted was to wash his hands of it and build a new life for himself. He succeeded, too."

"Was he happy?"

"I can't say for certain, but I imagine he found plenty of fulfillment. He served in the Peace Corps for a couple of years and did other volunteer work. It didn't matter where he went, he was liked by all. It's been said that he never met a man who didn't like him."

"Does this story have a punch line?" Amy asked, amused.

"Yes, I'm getting to that. Let me ask you a couple of questions first."

"All right." She'd come this far, and although she hadn't been a willing listener, her father had managed to whet her appetite.

"I want you to put yourself into this young man's place. Can you imagine how difficult it would be for him to approach his father eight years after this estrangement?"

"I'm confident he wouldn't unless there was a damn good reason."

"He had one. He'd fallen in love."

"Love?" Amy echoed.

"He did it for the woman, and for her father, too, I suspect. He knew a way to help them, and although it cost him everything, he went to his father and asked for help."

"I see," Any said, and swallowed tightly.

"Amy," he paused and held his hand out to her. "The company that made the offer, the company that *saved* us, is owned by Chance Powell, Josh's father."

Amy felt as if she had received a blow to the head. A ringing sensation echoed in her ears, and the walls started to circle the room in a crazy merry-go-round effect. "Josh went to his father for us?"

"You, sweetheart. He sold his soul for you."

Although Amy had been to New York several times, she had never appreciated the Big Apple as much as she did on this trip. The city was alive with the sights and sounds of Christmas. Huge boughs of evergreens were strung across the entryways to several major stores. The World Trade Center, always ablaze with lights, had never shone brighter. A stroll through Central Park made Amy feel like a child again.

Gone was the ever-present need to cry, replaced instead with a giddy happiness that gifted her with a deep, abiding joy for the season she hadn't experienced since the time she was a child and the center of her parents' world.

With the address clenched tightly in her hand, Amy walked into the huge thirty-story building that housed Chance Powell's brokerage. After making a few pertinent inquiries, she rode the elevator to the floor where his office was situated.

Her gaze scanned the neat row of desks, but she didn't see Josh, which caused her spirits to sag just a little. She'd come to find him, and she wasn't about to leave until she'd done exactly that.

"I'm here to see Mr. Powell," Amy told the receptionist. "I don't have an appointment."

"Mr. Powell is a very busy man. If you want to talk to him, I'm afraid you'll have to schedule a time."

"Just tell him Amy Johnson is here . . . you might add that I'm Harold Johnson's daughter," she added for good measure, uncertain that Josh had even mentioned her name.

Reluctantly, the young woman did as Amy said. No sooner had she said Amy's name than the office door opened and Chance Powell himself appeared. The resemblance between father and son was striking. Naturally, Chance's looks were mature, his dark hair streaked with gray, but his eyes were so like Josh's that for a moment it felt as if she was staring at Josh himself.

"Hello, Amy," he said, clasping her hands in both of his. His gaze slid over her appreciatively. "Cancel my ten o'clock appointment," he said to the receptionist.

He led the way into his office and closed the door. "I wondered about you, you know."

"I suppose that's only natural." Amy sat in the chair across from his rich mahogany desk, prepared to say or do whatever she must to find Josh. "I don't know what Josh said to you, if he explained—"

"Oh, he said plenty," the older man murmured and chuckled, seemingly delighted about something.

"I must find him," she said fervently, getting directly to the point.

"Must?"

Any ignored the question. "Do you know where he is?"

"Not at the moment."

"I see." Her hands tightened into a fist around the strap of her purse. "Can you tell me where I might start looking for him?" Her greatest fear was that he'd headed back to Kadiri or someplace else in the Middle East. It didn't matter, she would follow him to the ends of the earth if need be.

Chance Powell didn't seem inclined to give her any direct answers, although he had appeared eager enough to meet her. He scrutinized her closely, and he wore a silly half grin when he spoke. "My son always did have excellent taste. Do you intend to marry him?"

"Yes." She met his gaze head-on. "If he'll have me."

He laughed at that, boisterously. "Josh may be a good many things, but he isn't a fool."

"But I can't marry him until I can find him."

"Are you pregnant?"

Chance Powell was a man who came directly to the point, as well.

The color screamed in Amy's cheeks, and for a moment she couldn't find her tongue. "That's none of your business."

He laughed again, looking pleased, then slapped his hand against the top of his desk, scattering papers in several directions. "Hot damn!"

"Mr. Powell, please, can you tell me where I can find Josh? This is a matter of life and death." His death, if he didn't quit playing these games with her. Perhaps she'd been a fool to believe that all she had to do was fly to New York, find Josh and tell him how much she loved him so they could live happily ever after. It had never entered her mind that his father wouldn't know where he was. Then again, he may well be aware of precisely where Josh was at that very moment and not plan to tell her.

"Do you have any water?" she said, feigning being ill. "My... stomach's been so upset lately."

"Morning sickness?"

She blushed demurely and resisted the temptation to place the back of her hand to her brow and sigh with a good deal of drama.

"Please excuse me for a moment," Chance said, standing.

"Of course."

A moment turned out to be five long minutes, and when the office door opened, it slammed against the opposite wall and then was abruptly hurled closed. The sound was forceful enough to startle Amy out of her chair.

Josh loomed over her like a ten-foot giant, looking more furious than she could ever remember seeing him. His eyes were almost savage. "What the hell did you say to my father?"

"Hello, Josh," she said, offering him a smile he didn't return. Bracing her hands against the leather back of the chair, she used it as a shield between the two of them. The little speech she had so carefully prepared was completely lost. "I . . . I changed my mind about your offer. The answer is yes."

"Don't try to avoid the question," he shouted, advancing two steps toward her. "You told my father you're pregnant. We both know that's impossible."

He looked so good in a three-piece suit. So unlike the man who had asked to share a picnic table with her along the Seattle waterfront all those months ago. He had been wearing a fringed leather jacket then, and his hair had been in great need of a trim. Now . . . now he resembled a Wall Street executive, which was exactly what he was.

"What do you mean, you changed your mind?"

"I'm sorry I misled your father. I never came out directly and told him I was pregnant. But he didn't seem to want me to know where you were, and I had to find you."

"Why?"

He certainly wasn't making this easy on her. "Well, because . . ." she paused, drew in her breath and straightened her back, prepared for whatever followed. "Because I love you, Joshua Powell. I've reconsidered your marriage proposal, and I think it's a wonderful idea."

"The last I heard you were going to marry Chad Morton."

"That Milquetoast? Don't you know a bluff when you hear one?"

He frowned. "Apparently not."

"I want to marry *you*. I have from the day you first kissed me on the Seattle waterfront and then claimed it had been a mistake. We've both made several of those over the past months, but it's time to set everything straight between us. I'm crazy about you, Joshua Powell. Your father may be disappointed, but the way I figure it, we could make him and my father grandparents in about nine months. Ten at the tops.''

"Are you doing this out of gratitude?"

"Of course not," she said, as though the idea didn't even merit a response. "Out of love. Now please, stop looking at me as if you'd like to tear me limb from limb and come and hold me. I've been so miserable without you.''

He closed his eyes, and his shoulders and chest sagged. "Dear God, Amy..."

Unable to wait a moment longer, she walked into his arms the way a bird returns to its nest, without needing directions, recognizing home. A sense of supreme rightness filled her as she looped her arms around his neck and stood on her tiptoes. "I love you too, Angel Eyes," she said for him.

"I do, you know," he whispered, and his rigid control melted as he buried his face in her hair, rubbing his jaw back and forth against her temple as if drinking in her softness.

"There're going to be several children."

Fire hardened his dark eyes as he directed his mouth to hers in a kiss that should have toppled the entire thirty-story structure in which they stood. "How soon can we arrange a wedding?"

"Soon," she mumbled, her lips teasing his in a lengthy series of delicate, nibbling kisses. She caught his lower lip between her teeth and sucked at it gently, then offered him her tongue.

Josh fit his hand over the back of her head as he took control of the kiss, slanting his mouth over hers with a hungry demand that depleted her of all strength. Already a coil of sensation was tightening within her, and she circled her hips against him, delighting in his immediate response.

"You're playing with fire, angel," he warned softly, his dark eyes bright with passion.

She smiled up at him, her heart bursting with all the love she was experiencing. "I love it when you make dire predictions."

"Amy, I'm not kidding. Any more of that and you'll march to the altar a fallen angel."

She laughed softly. "Promises, promises."

Epilogue

"Amy?" Josh strolled in the back door of their home, expecting to find his pregnant wife either taking a nap or working in the nursery.

"I'm in the baby's room," he heard her shout from the top of the stairs.

Josh deposited his briefcase in the den, wondering why he even bothered to bring papers home to read. He had more entertaining ways of filling his evenings. Smiling, he mounted the stairs two at a time, while working loose the constricting silk tie at his neck. Even after five years, he still wasn't accustomed to working in a three-piece suit.

Just as he suspected, he discovered Amy with a tiny paintbrush in her hand, sketching a field of wildflowers around several large forest creatures on the nursery wall.

"What do you think?" she asked proudly.

Josh's gaze softened as it rested on her. "And to think I married you without ever knowing your many talents." He stepped back and observed the scene she was so busy creating. "What makes you so certain this baby is a boy?"

Her smile was filled with unquestionable confidence. "A woman knows these things."

Josh chuckled. "As I recall, you were equally confident Cain would be a girl. It was darn embarrassing, bringing him home from the hospital dressed entirely in pink."

"He's since forgiven me."

"Perhaps so, but I haven't." He stepped behind her and flattened his hands over her nicely rounded abdomen. Her stomach was tight and hard, and his heart fluttered with excitement at the thought of his child growing within her. "I can think of a way for you to make it up to me though," he whispered suggestively in her ear, then nibbled on her lobe. He felt her sag against him as he raised his hands from her abdomen to her breasts, cupping them.

"Joshua Powell, it's broad daylight."

"So?"

"So..."

He could tell she was battling more with herself than arguing with him. Josh hadn't known what to expect once they were married. He had heard rumors about women who shied away from their husbands after they had spoken their vows. But in all the years he had been married to Amy, she had greeted his lovemaking with an eagerness that made him feel humble and truly loved.

"Where's Cain? Napping?"

"No . . . he went exploring with my father," she whispered.

"Then we're alone?" He stroked her nipples suggestively, and his loins tightened at how quickly her body reacted to his needs. No matter how many times they made love, it was never enough, and it never would be. When he was ninety, he would be looking for a few private moments to steal away with her.

"Yes, we're the only ones here," she told him, her voice trembling just a little.

"Good." He kissed the curve of her neck, and she relaxed against him. He slid his hand to the waistband of her jeans and fiddled with the snap and zipper. He lowered it just enough to slip his hand inside her underwear, and down her lower abdomen until he found what he was seeking. She gave a soft cry of pleasure at his caress.

"Josh," she pleaded, breathless. "Let me clean the brush first."

He stroked the most sensitive part of her womanhood, feeling her almost immediate readiness. The years had taught him how to pleasure her, and he did so now until she was whimpering with need.

"Josh," she begged, moving against him, her small derriere massaging his erection in ways that served to heighten his arousal all the more. "Please," she moaned.

"I want to please you, angel, but you need to take care of that brush, remember."

"Oh, no, you don't," she cried softly. "You've got to take care of *me* first. You're the one who started this." Already she was removing her blouse, her fingers trembling, her hurried movements awkward. "I can't believe you," she cried, "in the middle of the day with Cain and my father due back any moment. We're acting like a couple of teenagers.''

"You make me feel seventeen again," Josh murmured. He released her and started undressing himself.

Amy locked the door, then turned and leaned against it, her hands behind her back. "I thought men were supposed to lose their sexual appetite when their wives were pregnant.''

Josh kicked off his shoes and removed his slacks. "Not me.''

"I noticed.''

He pinned her against the door, his forearms holding her head prisoner. "Do you have any complaints?''

"None," she whispered, framing his face lovingly with her hands. She kissed him, giving him her mouth and her tongue. She looped her arms around his neck as she moved her lush, sweet body against him, coming into intimate contact with his throbbing shaft.

They were both panting by the time Josh broke off the kiss. Amy worked her hands down and gripped his arousal between her hands. "It's so hot," she whispered. She touched him gently, creating and building such pleasure with the action of her fingers that Josh groaned and clenched his teeth. One solid stroke of her hand and he felt ready to explode.

"I want you," he managed.

"Right here?" Her eyes widened as they met his. "Now?''

He gripped her by the waist and raised her several inches off the ground, and then slowly lowered her so that he could enter her gently, without hurry.

Amy closed her eyes, sagged against the door and sighed.

"You okay?"

"Oh, yes," she whispered, and to prove just how okay she was, she arched her back and gently began to rotate her hips, enveloping him in a fever for which there was only one cure.

"Hold on, angel," he said, lifting her legs off the carpet until she was able to wrap them around his waist. With an eagerness he'd come to cherish from her, Amy met the impact of each of his thrusts. The sensual coil within him tightened unbearably. Amy found her release before he did, and his heart filled with love as she tossed back her head and made whimpering, catlike sounds that drove him past the point of control, and the whole universe exploded in a kaleidoscope of stars.

By the time Josh had drifted back to earth, Amy was spreading kisses all over his face. He marveled at her, this woman who was his wife. She was more woman than any man deserved, an adventurous lover, a helpmate, a friend, the mother of his children, a keel that brought balance to his existence and filled his life with purpose.

Gently he helped her dress, taking time to kiss and fondle her and tell her how much he loved her. Some things he had a difficult time saying, even now. Her love had taken all the bitterness from his life and replaced it with blessings too numerous to count.

As he bent over to retrieve his slacks, Josh placed a hand in the small of his back. "Remind me that I'm not seventeen the next time I suggest something like this."

"Not me," Amy murmured, tucking her arms around his neck and spreading kisses over his face. "That was too much fun. When can we do it again?"

"If you keep moving your breasts against me like that, it may be sooner than you think."

Amy kissed him, and as he wrapped his arms around the slight thickening at her waist, he closed his eyes to the surge of love that engulfed him.

"Come on," she said with a sigh, reaching for her paintbrush. "All this horsing around has made me hungry. How about some cream cheese and jalapenos spread over an English muffin?"

"No, thanks." His stomach quivered at the thought.

"It's good, Josh. Honest."

He continued to hold her to his side as they headed down the stairs. "By the way, my father phoned this afternoon," he mentioned casually. "He said he'd like to come out and visit before the baby's born."

Amy smiled at him. "You don't object?"

"No. It'll be good to see him. I think he'd like to be here for the baby's arrival."

"I think I'd like that, too," Amy said.

Josh nodded. He had settled his differences with his father shortly before he had married Amy. Loving her had taught him the necessity of bridging the gap. His father had made a mistake based on greed and pride, and that error had cost them both dearly. But Chance deeply regretted his actions, and had for years.

In his own way, Josh's father had tried reaching out to Josh through his sister-in-law, but he had never been able to openly confront Josh. However, when Josh had come to him, needing his help, Chance had been given the golden opportunity to make up to his son for the wrong he had done years earlier.

Amy set a roast in the oven and reached for an orange, choosing that over the weird food combination she'd mentioned earlier.

"Mommy, Mommy." Three-year-old Cain crashed through the back door and raced across the kitchen, his stubby legs pumping for all he was worth. "Grandpa and I saw a robin and a rabbit and a . . . a worm."

Josh waylaid his son, catching him under the arms and swinging him high above his head. "Where's Grandpa?"

"He said Mommy wouldn't want the worm inside the house so he put it back in the garden. Did you know worms live in the dirt and have babies and everything?"

"No kidding?" Amy asked, pretending to be surprised.

Harold Johnson came into the kitchen next, his face bright with a smile. "It looks like Cain gave you a run for your money, Dad," Amy said, kissing her father on the cheek. "I've got a roast in the oven, do you want to stay for dinner?"

"Can't," he said, dismissing the invitation. "I'm meeting the guys tonight for a game of pinochle." He stopped and looked at Josh. "Anything important happening at the office I should know about?"

"I can't think of anything offhand. Are you coming in on Tuesday for the board of directors' meeting?"

"Not if it conflicts with my golfing date."

"Honestly, Dad," Amy grumbled, washing her son's hands with a paper towel. "There was a time when nothing could keep you away from the business. Now you barely go into the office at all."

"Can't see any reason why I should. I've got the best CEO in the country. My business is thriving. Besides, I want to live long enough to enjoy my grandchildren. Isn't that right, Cain?"

"Right, Gramps." The toddler slapped his open palm against his grandfather's, then promptly yawned.

"Looks like you wore the boy out," Josh said, lifting Cain into his arms. The little boy laid his cheek on his father's shoulder.

"He'll go right down after dinner," Harold said, smiling broadly. "You two will have the evening alone." He winked at Josh and kissed Amy on the cheek. "You can thank me later," he whispered in her ear.

*   *   *   *   *

Silhouette Special Edition

COMING NEXT MONTH

#583 TAMING NATASHA—Nora Roberts
Natasha Stanislaski was a pussycat with Spence Kimball's little girl, but to Spence himself she was as ornery as a caged tiger. Would some cautious loving sheath her claws and free her heart from captivity?

#584 WILLING PARTNERS—Tracy Sinclair
Taking up residence in the fabled Dunsmuir mansion, wedding the handsome Dunsmuir heir and assuming instant ''motherhood'' surpassed secretary Jessica Lawrence's wildest dreams. But had Blade Dunsmuir wooed her for money...or love?

#585 PRIVATE WAGERS—Betsy Johnson
Rugged Steven Merrick deemed JoAnna Stowe a mere bit of fluff—until the incredibly close quarters of a grueling motorcycle trek revealed her fortitude *and* her womanly form, severely straining *his* manly stamina!

#586 A GUILTY PASSION—Laurey Bright
Ethan Ryland condemned his stepbrother's widow for her husband's untimely death. Still, he was reluctantly, obsessively drawn to the fragile-looking Celeste...and he feared she shared his damnable passion.

#587 HOOPS—Patricia McLinn
Though urged to give teamwork the old college try, marble-cool professor Carolyn Trent and casual coach C. J. Draper soon collided in a stubborn tug-of-war between duty...and desire.

#588 SUMMER'S FREEDOM—Ruth Wind
Brawny Joel Summer had gently liberated man-shy Maggie Henderson...body and soul. But could her love unchain him from the dark, secret past that shadowed their sunlit days of loving?

AVAILABLE THIS MONTH:

At long last, the books you've been waiting for by one of America's top romance authors!

DIANA PALMER
DUETS

Ten years ago Diana Palmer published her very first romances. Powerful and dramatic, these gripping tales of love are everything you have come to expect from Diana Palmer.

In March, some of these titles will be available again in DIANA PALMER DUETS—a special three-book collection. Each book will have two wonderful stories plus an introduction by the author. You won't want to miss them!

Book 1
SWEET ENEMY
LOVE ON TRIAL

Book 2
STORM OVER THE LAKE
TO LOVE AND CHERISH

Book 3
IF WINTER COMES
NOW AND FOREVER

Silhouette Books®

DP-1

You'll flip . . . your pages won't!
Read paperbacks *hands-free* with

Book Mate · I

The perfect "mate" for all your romance paperbacks

Traveling • Vacationing • At Work • In Bed • Studying
• Cooking • Eating

Perfect size for all standard paperbacks, this wonderful invention makes reading a pure pleasure! Ingenious design holds paperback books OPEN and FLAT so even wind can't ruffle pages — leaves your hands free to do other things. Reinforced, wipe-clean vinyl-covered holder flexes to let you turn pages without undoing the strap . . . supports paperbacks so well, they have the strength of hardcovers!

Pages turn WITHOUT opening the strap

SEE-THROUGH STRAP

Reinforced back stays flat.

Built in bookmark

BOOK MARK

BACK COVER HOLDING STRIP

10˝ x 7¼˝ opened.
Snaps closed for easy carrying, too

Available now. Send your name, address, and zip code, along with a check or money order for just $5.95 + .75¢ for postage & handling (for a total of $6.70) payable to Reader Service to:

Reader Service
Bookmate Offer
901 Fuhrmann Blvd.
P.O. Box 1396
Buffalo, N.Y. 14269-1396

Offer not available in Canada
*New York and Iowa residents add appropriate sales tax.

BM-G

❂ SILHOUETTE®

Desire™

Award of Excellence

Double the Excellence
Twice the Spice!

February is the month of love, and this month, *two* of your favorite authors have something terrific in store for you.

CONTACT by Lass Small
Ann Forbes had been burned in the past. But her determination to remain a solitary woman was *severely* tested by persistent Clint Burrows.

MAN OF THE MONTH

A LOVING SPIRIT by Annette Broadrick
Sabrina Sheldon never dreamed she had an angel on her side when she met sexy police officer Michael Donovan. He took her under his protective wings, and together their love soared....

These sizzling stories have merited the Award of Excellence and are available now from Silhouette Desire. Look for the distinctive emblem on the cover. It lets you know there's something truly special inside.

AEFEB-1

Silhouette Special Edition

proudly presents

Taming Natasha
by
NORA ROBERTS

In March, award-winning author Nora Roberts weaves her special brand of magic in TAMING NATASHA (SSE #583). Natasha Stanislaski was a pussycat with Spence Kimball's little girl, but to Spence himself she was as ornery as a caged tiger. Would some cautious loving sheath her claws and free her heart from captivity?

TAMING NATASHA, by Nora Roberts, has been selected to receive a special laurel—the Award of Excellence. Look for the distinctive emblem on the cover. It lets you know there's something truly special inside.

Available in March at your favorite retail outlet, or order your copy by sending your name, address, zip or postal code, along with a check or money order for $2.95, plus 75¢ postage and handling, payable to Silhouette Reader Service to:

In the U.S.
901 Fuhrmann Blvd.
Box 1396
Buffalo, NY 14269-1396

In Canada
P.O. Box 609
Fort Erie, Ontario
L2A 5X3

Please specify book title with your order.

TAME-1